T.

Arrival

of

Sherlock Holmes

A Truly Holmes Mystery

Jia Hartsiva

Cover image credit: Marisol Ibarra (background), Mohamed Hassan (woman), Gordon Johnson (skyline), and Clker-Free-Vector-Images (man) (on Pixabay). Other images: Mohamed Hassan (violin and question mark woman), Clker-Free-Vector-Images (magnifying glass) (on Pixabay).

ISBN: 978-1-7771660-1-4

*This book is dedicated to
my family and to those who are as passionate
about Sherlock Holmes as I am*

Table of Contents

Chapter 1 Sherlock Holmes

"You don't know Sherlock Holmes yet," he said; "perhaps you would not care for him as a constant companion."

—Sir Arthur Conan Doyle, *A Study in Scarlet*

As an English major and a classic literature cognoscenti, my head was usually filled with everything from the romances of Charlotte Brontë to the masterpieces of Oscar Wilde. Being in equal parts a history enthusiast, the reader can imagine my exhilaration when the university, during my first year of study, decided to buy the historic Baker House—an enormous three-storey Victorian home built in the 1850s and conveniently situated in the heart of downtown Toronto. I admit to being slightly infatuated with the place, for I walked by it almost daily, each time quivering with anticipation as it was slowly transformed into a student residence.

By the time my second year arrived, I had already applied for and secured one of the twenty spots that had opened at Baker House. Although my room was small and minimally furnished, I was too thrilled at the prospect of living in a space that held more than 150 years of history to care. It seemed I didn't know that history as well as my housemate, Sherlock Holmes.

Rumours about Holmes had already started fluttering about the place within days of moving in. Apparently, he was a third-year chemistry major, who had been expelled from his hometown university in London for cocaine possession. This wasn't too hard to believe. The first time I had caught a glimpse of him was through the open door to his room—he had sat crumpled in an old armchair with a look of stupor on his pale face, long arms and legs dangling lifelessly. I had fled the premises in alarm.

I soon realized that I preferred a lethargic Holmes to a cognizant one after our first conversation, which had been a startling experience to say the least.

I had been in our small, in-house library late one Saturday evening in September, perusing a volume of Anglo-Saxon poetry on the couch. The house was pleasantly silent since most of its occupants had left to do what ordinary college students did when the week was over. Sherlock Holmes was clearly as socially bizarre as I was since he looked noticeably disappointed when he strode into the library and saw that he would not have the space to himself.

"Watson, isn't it?" he asked in what would have been a charming British accent if his tone hadn't been so brusque. His hawkish, deep-set eyes darted to my shirt to which was pinned the laminated name tag that we had all been forced to wear since moving in.

"Janah Watson," I elaborated, feeling somewhat alarmed. No one had ever addressed me by my surname before without a polite "Miss" accompanying it. I recovered quickly though. "And you're —"

The scribble on his name tag was barely legible, but I had a feeling he had meant it to be that way. He took a moment to scrutinize me, but his face conveyed nothing but an odd smile, which made me wonder what he saw beyond my lanky form, caramel complexion, and long, black hair, which I habitually wore in a ponytail.

"Is there a place around here that serves a good steak and kidney pudding?" he asked, not bothering to introduce himself.

"The Village Idiot," I said, naming a quaint British pub about two blocks from Baker House.

"Excellent."

Having nothing further to say to me, Sherlock Holmes left to peruse the shelves, plucked a book from one of them a moment later (*The*

Handbook of Poisonous and Injurious Plants), and then sat on the loveseat adjacent to me, remaining silent for the next half hour.

I was quiet by nature with strangers and made no attempt at conversation. However, perhaps due to a lack of stimulation from elsewhere — my book of poems was anything but alluring — my attention settled on the tall, dark-haired outlander before me. At first, I snuck shy peeks, but eventually becoming dissatisfied with this, I stared blatantly and began my assessment. What I saw was a snow-white face garnished with a broad forehead, pointed nose, angular chin, and probing, grey eyes. He wasn't handsome in the conventional sense, but the intensity of his features compelled one's gaze to linger on him. Hence, my scrutiny continued beyond the face.

He had dressed his thin, six-foot frame in a white collared shirt, necktie, waistcoat, and dark pants, which looked rather odd in a college residence and made him appear older than he actually was. I thought he fit well with the old house, but our neighbours had smirked and snickered with little subtlety since his arrival. Thankfully, he was too immersed in his book to notice my prying gaze, and I soon returned to my poems, albeit grudgingly. The silence, however, wasn't destined to last.

"What a colourful history this house has!" Sherlock Holmes exclaimed, putting his book down.

Struck by his enthusiasm, I recited, "It was built in 1852 by a wealthy farmer named William Baker. He and his family lived here for more than thirty years before he passed away at the age of seventy-one." I wondered exactly what Holmes had found "colourful" about this history.

"Ah, an expert on Baker House. Brilliant! Then you must know that the family owned much of the surrounding land, farmed them, and had amassed quite a fortune by the time old Baker passed away." I nodded, and he went on, "And you must also know that something rather peculiar happened shortly after the man's death."

I thought for a moment. "Oh, the cow. Well, I wouldn't call it peculiar. There were reports that she'd been depressed days before Mr. Baker passed away in his sleep. It was as though she knew what was going to happen. A bit romantic actually."

"Oh, I am certain the cow was depressed. That is, in fact, the word I would use to describe this whole wicked affair. Depressing! By the way, the murder of a cow and its master is anything but romantic."

I blinked, unsure whether I had understood him correctly. "Murder?"

Much to my disappointment, no elaboration was offered. Instead, Holmes said, "Tell me all you know about Baker and his cow. Perhaps a recitation of the facts out loud will allow you to see what I see."

"Um, okay." I cleared my throat, suddenly feeling uncomfortable as a pair of unblinking eyes stared at me. "That cow—her name was Bella—was Mr. Baker's favourite. Bella was born on the farm, and he helped raise her. His preference went so far that he only drank her milk. After he passed away, his family found Bella dead a few days later. They say she died of heartbreak."

Holmes greeted my story of compassion with a hideously mocking laugh. "Romantic indeed. Filling your head with poetic rubbish is clearly interfering with your ability to think logically," he said, gesturing at my book. Then, without warning, he stood up and replaced my book with his before sitting down again. "And now let us return to the double murder. That is your hint." He nodded at the volume that now weighed heavily against my thighs.

I stared at the book and then at him incredulously. "Are you saying Mr. Baker and his cow were poisoned?"

"Yes!"

"But that's ridiculous!"

"Pshaw! I think not. Shall I name the poison?" Without waiting for an answer or pausing for breath, he continued, "The white snakeroot, a deadly plant native to eastern and central North America. You are not familiar with it? Why, it was the plant that killed US president Abraham

Lincoln's mother! I can't believe you have never heard—"

I said nothing but frowned, which perhaps encouraged Holmes to quit his disparaging rant.

"Anyway, as a seasoned farmer and amateur botanist, William Baker would have known better than to allow the plant to proliferate on the lands his livestock grazed on. No, I reckon it was secretly introduced to Bella, whose milk then became contaminated with its toxin and passed on to her master. Snakeroot is toxic to humans and cattle, and both victims perished accordingly. Hm, you look skeptical."

I tried my best to extinguish all traces of disbelief on my face—out of politeness, of course—and attempted to pacify him. However, Holmes didn't seem offended at all. Before I could speak, he chuckled loudly and carried on in a feverishly animated manner that was beginning to unnerve me.

"Good of you not to blindly accept everything you hear. You want proof, and I shall provide it. You know, I was afraid I would be stuck in a house full of idiots for the next two years, but there appears to be some hope. Now, allow me to compel you." He pulled out a smartphone, unlocked it, tapped the screen a few times, and then thrust it into my hand. "Have a look. Go on, look!"

On the screen was a photo of the front page of an old newspaper dated to the 1880s—the *Morning Telegraph*. Much of the page was filled with a monochromatic image of a bulbous man and an even larger cow, neither of whom looked very happy — that is, if it were possible for cows to look discontent in a photograph.

"Where did you — "

"I visited the university library's newspaper archives and was quite pleased to find this. William Baker was popular enough in the community to make the front page when he died. This photo was taken a few days before his death, which makes it quite valuable to the investigator. Now, look closely at the cow. Rather strange, wouldn't you say?"

I shrugged. "All I see is a cow."

"You see, but you do not observe."

I stared harder, then looked up helplessly at my strange companion.

After an impatient "humph", the following was imparted in a tone that clearly suggested that one unequipped with such knowledge was an idiot: "One of the symptoms of snakeroot poisoning in animals is depression, which obviously cannot be perceived from a photo, but the anecdotal record you mentioned supports this. Next, note Bella's arched back and how her hind legs are placed quite close together. Cows don't naturally stand like this. This is yet another indication. Had we been present in 1883 when Baker died, we would have no doubt seen some of the other symptoms as well, like excessive saliva production and breathing troubles."

"I think Bella is salivating in this photo," I said, zooming in on the cow's mouth, and received a nod of approval for this. "I'm guessing you also have a suspect in mind?"

"The son-in-law, George Wood, of course. He stood to gain the most and inherited everything once the old man died as Baker had no sons. You will recall that Wood sold the land lot by lot and retired a wealthy man." Holmes sighed unhappily. "The problem with solving cases from over a century ago is that one cannot apprehend the perpetrator. It is rather unsatis — why are you looking at me like that?"

I blinked, unsure of how to formulate a response that would not offend the man I was to share a home with for the foreseeable future. But the entire notion was stupefying! Did he think he could rewrite history based on a few trivial details from an old photograph? The unnerving twinkle in his eyes made me question his sanity. If he were as sane as I, then I blamed his arrogance for my mixed feelings of irritation and anxiety.

"Uh, thank you for the — uh — interesting exercise," I began politely, "but I think I'll stick to what the history books say."

The melancholy from just moments before vanished, and a cold glare spread across the man's pale features. The hiss that emerged teemed with impatience and a gingerly controlled anger. "Your loss," he muttered.

My exasperation grew. "You can't just take random, little details and recreate the truth!"

"There is but one truth. It cannot be recreated. It can only be revealed, which is precisely what I just did through observation and deduction."

"But you can't prove your theory."

"Too late for that, but that doesn't invalidate what I am saying. I have my method, and it is based on the observation of *random, little details*." He stressed the last three words in a sardonic fashion, then his lips curved into a mischievous sneer. "Perhaps I can offer you a personalized demonstration?"

I raised an eyebrow but remained silent.

"You are of Indian ancestry through your mother's side."

I nodded, unimpressed, since a single glance at me and my name tag made this observation an obvious one. Perhaps he had even noticed my Indian flag keychain, a trinket that had once belonged to my grandmother. What followed, however, was admittedly remarkable.

"You are an English major, attending university on a scholarship. You are poor, possibly an orphan, you fancy books over people, and you are quite fond of Victorian-era architecture and long walks."

"How did you know all that?" I cried in astonishment.

His response didn't come right away, but my awe-struck outburst had appeased his sour mood considerably. In fact, he chuckled and seemed to savour my impatience.

"This is not a library book," he finally said, fingering the spine of *Anglo-Saxon Poetry*, "as it is missing the yellow sticker indicative of university property. It is brand new, purchased recently. You bought it but not for pleasure; you grimaced more than once while reading it. That clearly demonstrates that it is for a course. You aren't a fan of poetry, but you took the class anyway, which tells me that it is a requirement for your degree. Hence, an English major."

"The scholarship and my financial status?"

Holmes smiled. "The pitfall of our age cohort is an inclination towards haute couture, regardless of whether one is rich or poor. I've spotted twenty-seven designer handbags in this residence over the past couple of days, and yet there are only thirteen female residents. Startling, isn't it? You, on the other hand, possess none. The worn state of your clothes and the desperate state of your shoes, which also indicates that you walk a lot, tell me that you are not financially well off. Yet you have no part-time job and can afford tuition and to live on campus. Hence, a scholarship."

"How do you know I don't have a job?"

"Simple. Today is Saturday. Baker House is practically empty because half of our neighbours are flipping burgers or waiting tables and the rest are at a pub. Here you are, sitting in our neglected library, doing neither.

That tells me you have no job and prefer books over people."

I laughed. The reasoning was so simple that my initial astonishment dissipated immediately. "It all seems very obvious now that you've explained it. Anyone could do this."

Holmes sighed. "*Omne ignotum pro magnifico.*" Seeing my blank expression, which clearly communicated that I knew not a word of Latin, he explained, "'Everything unknown seems magnificent.' I ought to keep the explanations to myself."

I grinned, then said, "For the record, I'm not an orphan. I have an older brother, but he doesn't live here. My parents died in a car crash when I was six, and my grandmother raised us. She passed away last year, and I moved to the city."

"So you are quite alone." After a pause, he murmured, "Like me."

I wanted to pry for more details, but a single glance at his brooding expression stifled this urge. Instead, I said, "Why did you think I was an orphan?"

"No phone calls from family, no care packages, and no mention of them while you conversed with our neighbours. I supposed that you were either extremely reserved or had no family to talk about."

Although I tried to mask the alarm in my voice, it seeped out. "You've been watching me?"

Sherlock Holmes chuckled. "I watch everything and everyone. Unfortunately, there are very few persons of interest in this house. Now, shall I continue my demonstration? Hm, ah, yes, your love of Victorian architecture — quite apparent, that one. You could have picked any of the residences to live in — I hear the new one just two blocks up the street has a heated swimming pool — but here you are."

"You're here as well."

"Quite so. I feel an inexplicable warmth in the presence of wooden panelling and fireplaces. I feel at home here in this house." He stood. "I think I need a cigarette now. Ah, you detest cigarettes. Yes, it is an ugly habit, but the alternative is cocaine."

He didn't see my look of horror since he had already turned towards the exit. Once at the door, he spun around.

"I forgot to mention that although you are intelligent enough to win a scholarship, you are also extremely gullible. You believed a cow died of heartbreak after all. Quite absurd, if you ask me. I wonder if you will say ghosts are real too." He paused. "My name is Holmes, by the way. Sherlock Holmes. But you already knew that." And with that, he was off.

I remained sitting for an entire five minutes after he had left. Slowly, I rose, retook possession of *Anglo-Saxon Poetry*, which lay discarded on the seat, sat back down, and began reading. When I left the library an hour later, I took Holmes' book with me.

*

Over the next couple of days, Sherlock Holmes entertained and, in a few cases, mortified the residents of Baker House with some extraordinary observations and fantastical deductions that sometimes led to uncomfortable truths. In fact, several of these truths emerged: Mariah Murphy's boyfriend was cheating on her, Rita Gopal found it thrilling to shoplift, and Rory Moffatt sold drugs. Each of these declarations was followed by a simple explanation that drew attention to some minute detail no one had noticed. This impressed only the old cleaning lady, Mrs. Martha Hudson. Consequently, Holmes spoke to her more often than his fellow students, most of whom civilly ignored him. A nasty few sometimes gave him a rough push, opportunely timed when he was carrying his morning coffee.

One morning, I had found him in our communal kitchen, helping himself to a second cup of coffee since the contents of his first had been splattered violently across his crisp white shirt. His face, I could see, was flushed, and his lips were pressed into a thin, angry line. His eyes pierced mine, then softened.

"*Wir sind gewohnt, daß die Menschen verhöhnen, was sie nicht verstehen,*" he said quietly. "Simply put, people mock what they do not understand. Such a shame, isn't it?"

"Maybe you should take a self-defence class? Wrestling or boxing?" I suggested helpfully, although I didn't think his slim frame could handle either sport.

Holmes, however, looked thoughtful as he left the kitchen. I didn't know whether he pursued my suggestion or not. Perhaps he had realized that staying out of sight was easier than boxing, for he soon left the house only for classes and swiftly retreated to his room, spending hours in there and emerging only for meals, which he often took back to his sanctum sanctorum. He frequently acknowledged me with a curt nod, which I always returned. On more than one occasion, he entered the library in the evenings to find me curled up there with a book. With both of us being naturally unsociable and reticent, we shared the space wordlessly, a simple nod serving as both "hello" and "goodbye".

By the time a windy October arrived, our quiet liaison had evolved to include bits of conversation. I had thought Holmes peculiar prior to this, but he turned out to be far more eccentric than I had anticipated.

If one were to have a brief conversation with him, they would be struck by his antiquated attitude and plethoric, old-fashioned speech. A lengthier discussion would have revealed his expertise on select subjects, which included chemistry, anatomy, law, and some botany as demonstrated by the white snakeroot incident.

He also occasionally inserted bits of Latin, French, and German into conversations, so it was safe to assume that he had at least a rudimentary knowledge of these languages. The number of arcane facts he managed to store in his head was remarkably large, if not outright unnatural. He explained this seemingly unattainable ability by introducing me to the "brain attic".

"The key, Watson, is to keep your brain attic in pristine condition," he said one afternoon. "You are filling yours with rubbish." Here, he nodded at the copy of *Wuthering Heights* in my hands.

Unlike myself, Holmes had no interest in literature and often mocked my attraction to fiction. He had, with little subtlety, recommended on more than one occasion that I switch my studies to something more practical. That day, I had been more perplexed by the new terminology to be disputatious, and so I had decided to forgive the insult and inquire for an explanation.

"You see," he began, "the brain is like an empty attic. You have to stock it as you choose. A fool will fill it with information pertaining to everything he or she comes across, so that the knowledge that might be useful to them gets lost in the rubble or mixed up with a lot of other things. Hence, they are unable to find what they are looking for. It is very important not to have useless facts elbowing out the useful ones."

Holmes preferred to fill his brain attic with the details of a century's worth of true crimes — a pastime which I found disturbing to say the least. The usefulness of this was beyond me, but he seemed to think it was a good use of his time to do so.

Co-habitation revealed further perplexing oddities. For instance, he was prone to mood swings to an almost concerning degree, being sulky one day and energetic the next. Putrid smells seeped out of his room since he liked to experiment with chemicals from the comfort of his desk. He smoked too often to suit my taste, but luckily, I had not caught him doing anything more dangerous. When nicotine failed to stimulate him, he turned to playing the violin, which he preferred to do late at night. He played beautifully though and so I tolerated it. The rest of Baker House did not, and I surmised he did it to irritate them.

I came to understand that his was a higher intelligence. His deductions never ceased to amaze me, but we argued incessantly since he had a tendency to infantilize me by ridiculing my reasonings and making me beg for answers. In an odd sort of way, I found our relationship, which sat somewhere between friendship and rivalry, engaging.

The truth was that I had grown used to Sherlock Holmes, although I denied it adamantly. This was possibly why on one Saturday evening two weeks before Halloween, after attempting in vain to finish an assignment, I pushed away my laptop and went in search of Holmes.

I found him in the parlour by a moonlit window, his body arranged in a peculiar manner on a purple mat. His hands and feet were flat on the ground, holding up the rest of his body, which formed a steep inverted V. Between his hands lay a newspaper, which he appeared to be reading. Watching him from a corner of the room were two of our fellow housemates. They were tall, beefy, and red-faced; the latter trait was possibly due to the contents of their cups, which yielded a scent strong enough to be smelled from across the room. I suspected they were *not* drinking orange juice. Fearing that their matching mischievous grins foreshadowed something unpleasant in store for Holmes, I scurried forward.

Upon reaching Holmes, I noticed with some amusement that he had traded his old-fashioned wardrobe for a pair of shorts and a T-shirt. For a moment, he looked like every other guy who lived at Baker House, but then he opened his mouth and the effect crumbled.

"*Adho Mukha Svanasana*," he announced in a voice that flowed out effortlessly even though his head hung low, sandwiched between his arms.

"Yeah, most of us know it as downward dog," I muttered, then stood awkwardly, unsure of what to say next.

Holmes slowly straightened his body and transitioned into a plank pose. He said nothing and made no effort to stand up, his attention still occupied by the newspaper. Finally, realizing that I hadn't left, he spoke, although his eyes remained on the ground.

"The weather is supposed to be warm tomorrow. Do you fancy going for a cuppa in the afternoon? I believe I have finally discovered a café that doesn't sell mediocre coffee."

I was so startled by the unexpected invitation that I nodded promptly. What a naive girl I was.

Chapter 2 The Lamenting Lady

"She is more like a ghost than a woman."
—Sir Arthur Conan Doyle, *A Study in Scarlet*

HAD I KNOWN THAT I WOULD BE VISITING ONE OF the city's most affluent neighbourhoods, I may have made an effort to dress nicely — that is, not wear a pair of corduroy overalls that still had paint stains from the time I helped renovate my grandmother's kitchen two years ago. Unfortunately, I had failed to notice the splotches while dressing the following morning.

We left the deserted university grounds shortly after ten o'clock and walked for some time before grabbing drinks — black coffee (ugh!) for Holmes and a maple latte with a mountain of whipped cream for me — at a quaint, little bakery at the corner of Esley and Bloor Streets. I would have preferred to linger in the shop for an hour or two, where the air was sweet with the aromas of pastries and coffee, but it seemed Holmes was eager to embrace the autumn chill again and walk amid skyscrapers and pedestrians. In silence, we resumed the leisurely pace of our fellow strollers and headed north on Esley. Holmes eventually crossed a bridge that led us down a quiet street lined with large homes, each more opulent than the next. I followed, becoming more and more conscious of my attire the further we walked, but refused to protest. As a compromise, I zipped up my jacket, which was a smart move since my exposed neck was starting to turn pink.

We reached the end of the road and turned onto a winding street lined with even larger houses, some of whose patrons had put up stunning Halloween decorations, including a gigantic, plastic bat that hung from the face of one home. As the last bit of the busy Bloor Street disappeared behind us and the vicinity turned entirely residential, my sense of direction started to waver. Wordlessly, I let Holmes carve a path for us, for he was clearly heading somewhere. He offered no explanation, however, and broke the silence only once to say, "This was one of the first neighbourhoods in your town to have curved streets. Did you know that, Watson?"

"A town? We're not a town! The population is in the millions!"

Holmes shrugged. "Feels like a town compared to London."

The walk carried on in silence after that. Unsurprisingly. Twenty minutes later, I had nearly convinced myself that Holmes took walks like normal people when he suddenly stopped.

Before us was a gated estate. The gate was open though, and I could see a paved path leading to a large, two-storey house of crimson brickwork with a nearly symmetrical façade of arched windows, small balconies, and a garage. A grand, mahogany door, flanked by four slender Greek columns, added to the air of antique-like opulence. The lawn was less impeccable though; above the bright, artificial greenery lay a great number of dead leaves. A sign boasting the name of a security alarm company stood nearby.

"We have arrived," Sherlock Holmes announced, and stepped onto the property as though he owned the place. I lingered for a moment, cheeks flushed, as I eyed his long, grey wool coat and brown, leather Oxfords and compared them to my own batty appearance. Realizing the absence of my footsteps behind him, Holmes turned around brusquely and motioned me to come. Now noticing his neat collared shirt and cardigan, I suppressed a growl and followed him grudgingly.

Despite marching onto the property, Holmes did have the courtesy to ring the bell, although, in retrospect, I supposed he did that only because he lacked the ability to walk through solid wood.

"What are we doing here?" I asked while we waited.

"Mrs. H has reported a series of outré occurrences in this house and wishes for my help in getting to the bottom of it." Before I could ask how Mrs. Hudson knew folks who could afford a home worth millions of dollars, Holmes continued, "Mrs. H used to be this family's live-in housekeeper. The present housekeeper, Roksanda Dragomirov, approached her for help. Mrs. H has always been appreciative of my capabilities and thought that I would be the perfect candidate to investigate this little problem. She is waiting for us inside."

"You investigate things?"

Holmes grinned. "Oh, yes! It would be a waste of my skills if I didn't apply them in some productive way. I fancy myself a sleuth-hound."

"And you've carried out these—er— investigations before?"

"Of course. My clientele consisted of fellow university students back in London. This will be my first case here, and you will have the grand privilege of assisting me. Quite exciting, eh! This town is not as bleak as I thought it would be."

Irked by the mention of "town" again, I opened my mouth to protest when Holmes, having grown impatient from waiting, tried the doorknob, and finding that it turned, opened the door and entered the house.

We found ourselves in a foyer that was nearly three times the size of my bedroom at Baker House. Although the lights were off, bright sunlight poured in from two tall, cathedral-style windows and illuminated nearly every inch of the space. Much to my delight, the room was lined with wooden walls and decorated with a stylish mix of both modern and old-fashioned furniture. A black velvet ottoman bench sat nearby, and to our left a bright red parka and a large brown coat hung on a sturdy-looking coat rack. We deposited our jackets there, although it wouldn't have been too far-fetched to anticipate the arrival of a stooping butler to whisk away our belongings. Hardwood floors peaked from beneath a circular taupe rug with intricate floral patterns. Hanging from the cream pearl ceiling was the most magnificent chandelier I had ever seen; it glittered handsomely despite not being lit. To our right, a spacious staircase snaked along the wall, its polished wooden steps leading up to the unlit second-floor landing.

And that was where my gaze came to rest.

The light from the foyer windows managed to just touch the landing, allowing me to sense movement beyond the handrail. At first glance, it seemed as though some vague shape was flitting about, constantly emerging from and blending into the darkness. I managed to make out only one thing—a thick coil of rope. The shadow threw a part of the rope over the handrail and a struggle of some sort ensued. I heard a very faint whimper. Just as I realized that the shadow was a person, a woman climbed over the handrail, now fully exposed by the light.

The apparition seemed so surreal that I wondered for a moment if we were in the company of a ghost. The woman's sickly face, framed by her long, dark hair, and the flowing, white dress that wrapped her measly body were highly suggestive. From what I could see of her face, she appeared to be in her late thirties, but her small, emaciated body seemed as though it belonged to either someone much younger or many decades older. The pallor of her skin looked unhealthy, and her thin lips were stretched into a grimace. My eyes were transfixed on hers, which were incredibly large and eerily vacant. My attention then fell on the rope that coiled like a snake around her neck. Horrified, I saw that the other end of it had been tied to the handrail.

"Holmes," I whispered, "she won't actually jump, right?"

"Oh, I am certain she will," came the hushed response.

Now I knew with certainty that the woman standing a storey above us, hovering between life and death, was real—Holmes could see her too. "How do you know that?"

"There is sadness on her face, Watson. She will jump any minute now."

"What do we do?"

There was no reply. Instead, Holmes took a daring step forward and said loudly, "Ma'am, you need to stop what you are doing."

The woman seemed not to hear, for she looked straight ahead, completely unaware of her audience. I stared at her, tempted to avert my gaze in case the worst happened but unable to do so.

"Dr. Aurelia Richardson, you need to get back on the landing," Holmes commanded in a remarkably authoritative voice. The name, and perhaps the tone of the command, surprised the woman as much as it did me. She jerked out of her trance and looked down at us, finally aware of our presence, but her ashen fingers made no attempt to loosen the rope. Instead, she shook her head sadly.

"I'm so sorry," she said, now weeping. "I was supposed to die this way. The Place predicted it. Everybody else died. Why should I be the only one to be spared?"

None of this made sense to me, and a single look at Holmes told me that he was in the dark as well. I stepped away from the centre of the foyer as quietly as I could. The woman named Aurelia Richardson was staring too intensely at Holmes to notice that I had slipped onto the staircase and begun my ascent. Holmes noticed, of course. Judging by the way his body stiffened,

I was sure he thought that my interference would cause the woman to jump. I was afraid of that too, but something had to be done. A single step could end everything, and I would be forever haunted by visions of a hanging woman.

My heroics came to an abrupt stop, however, when another shadow appeared on the landing some distance behind the woman. Twice the size of her meager form, it took very slow, deliberate steps towards her, which made my anxiety peak; I wasn't sure if the figure would save Aurelia or trigger her deathly dive.

It felt like entire minutes had elapsed before I regained control of my paralyzed feet, but as soon as I had taken a step, the shadow lurched forward and grabbed Aurelia. She gave out a frantic cry. In one swift motion, it had pulled her over the handrail, and both woman and shadow disappeared into obscurity. I rushed onto the landing with Holmes trailing me to discover Aurelia sprawled on the floor with a large thing keeping her pinned down.

Somehow, in the midst of this confusing ruckus, Holmes managed to find the light switch rather than become distracted by the squirming figures like me. The lights came on, momentarily baffling Aurelia and her rescuer. Now that the landing had been illuminated, I could see that what had appeared as a massive, intimidating silhouette just moments before was, in fact, a young man—tall, broad-shouldered, and well-built, with tanned skin and small, dark eyes framed by closely cropped black hair. Aurelia looked like a child in his grip. Perhaps she had realized how futile it was to struggle because she soon went limp and began sobbing softly as the man untied the rope around her neck.

"What's going on here?" bellowed a deep voice.

I turned around just as a tall, brawny man with a shock of white hair shot past me and almost violently untangled Aurelia and pulled her to her feet. As his arms wrapped protectively around her, his dark eyes fell on the rope, which now hung limply from the handrail. His bushy eyebrows furrowed and his lips thinned in anger as he watched the other man slowly climb to his feet.

"Alejo, what is the meaning of this?" he barked.

The man named Alejo stared speechlessly for a moment before replying weakly in accented English, "Mr. Richardson, I don't know what happened. I left her in her room for only a few minutes, sir. I don't know where she got the rope from."

"Your job is to look after her twenty-four hours a day, seven days a week. What was so important that you had to step out?"

Alejo's face reddened as he mumbled a few words, two of which I understood to be "smoke break". Mr. Richardson, who I assumed was Aurelia's father, turned crimson as well. Some foul-mouthed words appeared to be on the tip of his tongue when he noticed Holmes and me. His acknowledgement, however, consisted of only a nod, and then his attention returned to Alejo.

"Take Aurelia to the kitchen," he said, lips quivering from stifled anger. "Have Roksanda prepare something warm for her to drink. I'll be down in a minute."

Aurelia squirmed in protest, pressing herself against his chest. "No, daddy. Not him, not him. His grip is as tight as the noose that wrapped around my neck in that forest," she whimpered.

Mr. Richardson sighed, then murmured something into his daughter's ear and embraced her tenderly. "I'll join you in just a minute, love. Now go on." He gave Alejo a stern nod, and soon Aurelia could be seen clambering down the stairs unhappily with her caregiver.

Mr. Richardson finally turned to us. "Alistair Richardson," he said, extending a hand. "I assume that you're here at Martha's request."

Holmes nodded, although his gaze was fixed on the rope instead of the man. I gave him a nudge, and proper introductions were made. Holmes got straight to the point.

"Mrs. H explained that your daughter, Dr. Richardson, has been at the centre of some bizarre happenings, but she didn't elaborate. Before I begin my investigation, I will need the entire story."

Mr. Richardson gave us a stare as severe as the one Alejo had received just moments before. "I personally don't like the idea of strangers investigating my family, especially when my daughter's health is so sensitive." He studied us boldly, very much unsatisfied with what he saw. Then, he sighed. "But Martha seems to trust you, and I trust her judgement. She raised my girls, so I know she would act in their best interest. I trust that you'll use discretion here."

Holmes nodded. "What has been going on in this house, Mr. Richardson?"

"What you just saw—that's what's been happening here since September."

The next question that emerged from Holmes was rather blunt. I could have thought of a thousand ways of asking it more civilly, but it seemed politeness was not one of Holmes' strong suits when his mind was hungry for information.

"What is wrong with Dr. Richardson?" he demanded.

Mr. Richardson seemed more saddened than angered by the pointedness of the question. "Thirty-nine years old—she should've been married with a couple of kids and a solid career. She had all that six years ago, but that—that man—" He struggled for a moment, refraining from no doubt unpleasant words to describe someone he found despicable. "Her husband— ex-husband—I always knew he wasn't good enough for her—he left her, and she became an alcoholic. She lost custody of my granddaughter."

He paused, looking bitter, before going on. "I thought losing Casey would motivate her to get her life back on track, and it did for a time. She was a biological anthropologist, you know. Her last excavation took her to Africa a-and that's when it went downhill again." Here, his voice broke, and he shook his head as though ridding himself of something dreadful. "She suffered a mental breakdown and had to be put in an institution for over five years. But she got better. She moved in with us earlier this year, and I hired Alejo as her nurse. Things were fine for a while. She was distant, but she wasn't delirious."

"So what happened?" Holmes asked.

"I don't know," came the man's disheartened reply. "Last month, Aurelia became agitated. Every little thing frightened her. She believed that she was being haunted."

"By whom, if I may ask?"

Mr. Richardson blinked. "S-she didn't say."

Holmes eyed the man suspiciously for a moment. I was inclined to think he hadn't believed Mr. Richardson's stuttered response. He didn't delve on the topic of phantoms, however, and soon went on with his interrogation.

"You are certain nothing triggered her relapse?"

"Nothing that I can think of. She's been taking her medication. Her doctors don't understand what happened."

"Why not have her institutionalized again?"

"Because—" Again, Mr. Richardson's voice broke, and anguish distorted his features. "I can't bear to do that to her again. She was well and now she isn't, but it's not her. Something strange is going on."

Holmes raised an eyebrow. "Do you believe that your daughter is indeed being haunted?"

"No, that's ridiculous."

The questioning tone of his voice didn't convince me, but I remained silent out of politeness. Holmes did not, and when he spoke, there was a sneering quality to his voice.

"Perhaps a ghost tied this rope to the handrail in an attempt to lure your daughter to her death?"

Mr. Richardson's lips thinned in anger. "Look, I can't explain it, but something is stopping Aurelia from getting better. That's all I know."

Although Mr. Richardson's ire had made a herculean man like Alejo the nurse tremble, Holmes looked rather unfazed as he coolly said, "I think you know much more. There is, for example, an immense sadness burdening your daughter. What can you tell me about that?"

"Sadness? Why would you think that?"

"I saw her face, Mr. Richardson, as she stood on the landing. The corners of her lips were pulled down, and the inner corners of her eyebrows were raised — classic signs of sadness. The latter, in particular, is difficult for most to do at will. Hence, your daughter is languishing about something, and it nearly drove her to suicide."

But Mr. Richardson shook his head adamantly. "That's nonsense. There's nothing for her to be sad about."

We would not hear anything more on the subject from him, although judging by the way he refused to meet our eyes, I was certain the whole story hadn't been disclosed. Realizing the interrogation had come to an end, Holmes abruptly turned his attention to the rope and knelt to examine it.

"Is Dr. Richardson right-handed?" he asked a moment later. The answer was in the affirmative. "Pooh! That is of no help. This rope was tied by a right-handed person — or perhaps a right-handed ghost." He chuckled softly as he peered at the rope again. His assessment — a process that consisted of feeling the texture, tugging and poking at the knot, and finally, sniffing it — continued for another minute. He then straightened, wearing a peculiar look.

"The ghost is not bloodthirsty. How curious!"

Naturally, Mr. Richardson and I were alarmed by this exclamation. Unfortunately for our curiosities, no explanation could be provided, since at that precise moment, a petrified howl filled the air.

Mr. Richardson shot past us and ran down the stairs with a vitality that astonished me, even though it was obvious that his sturdy frame was more than capable of outrunning me any day. We were quick to follow and soon found ourselves running across the foyer and down a hallway that led to the back of the house. Aurelia lay in the middle of this hallway, half-sprawled on the hardwood floor and partly pressed against the wall. Her eyes were shut tight. The nurse, Alejo, was tugging at her arm. She, however, was adamantly refusing to move forward, although I couldn't see what could have bothered her so much. The familiar face of Mrs. Martha Hudson greeted us with a solemn nod. She was squatting next to Aurelia and stroking her hair tenderly; the expression on her face was so mournful that I felt a terrible melancholy in return.

"I can't," Aurelia was saying as we reached her. "Just take it down, please." Her face had barely dried from the episode upstairs. Now fresh tears slid down her gaunt cheeks, and she was shaking her head fanatically.

Mr. Richardson glared at Alejo as though this was somehow his fault, then pleaded to his daughter, "Aurelia, please. It's just a painting." The words had no effect on her though; her eyes sprang open, and she shot a wild glance at the portraits and paintings that decorated the opposite wall. This seemed to provoke a fresh outburst and prompted her gaze to lower before

I could discern which of the works had caused her so much grief.

"It's the Place," she wailed. "I see their bones every time I look at those woods. You need to burn it! Burn it!"

Chapter 3 Delusions and Deductions

"I am simply applying to ordinary life a few of those precepts of observation and deduction which I advocated in that article."

—Sir Arthur Conan Doyle, *A Study in Scarlet*

NEITHER ALEJO'S VIGOROUS TUGGING NOR MR. Richardson's soothing murmurs persuaded Aurelia to continue her passage down the hallway. The two men were left with no choice but to forcibly drag her along the floor. The poor woman cried loudly and struggled without tiring, shutting her eyes tightly as the trio passed the artwork. Just as they reached the end of the hallway, Mr. Richardson, unable to keep his hold on Aurelia's wriggling arm, let go. Judging by his look of anguish, I suspected that he released her intentionally, unable to bear the fact that his grip was causing his daughter a great deal of pain. Unfortunately, Aurelia's flailing hand knocked over a tall, wooden display stool that held a table lamp.

The deafening bang that sounded as the lamp struck the floor brought forth a thin woman, with short, blond hair and an excessive amount of neck, from one of the doors that opened into the hallway. She looked about fifty, although the deep halter neckline of the velvet jumpsuit she was wearing contradicted my guess. One would have estimated an age of twenty-five, at least below the neck. Her green eyes were amplified by oversized glasses, and her dark, penciled eyebrows contrasted sharply with the rest of her pale face. At the sight of the shattered lamp, her eyes grew comically large, giving her the appearance of a tarsier. Then, her gaze fell on Aurelia, and her nose crinkled as though she were plagued by an unpleasant smell.

"She didn't just do that!" the woman shrieked. "It was vintage! An ivory bell shade! She just destroyed a priceless treasure!"

Mr. Richardson cast a woeful glance at the woman, who I assumed was his wife. As she stormed back into the room she had emerged from, he looked pitifully at his weeping daughter, gave Mrs. Hudson a nod, and then wordlessly followed Mrs. Richardson. Everything was still for a moment after the door slammed shut. Then, heated, muffled voices sounded. This, unfortunately, worsened Aurelia's agitation. Alejo quickly resumed control of her hand and managed to drag the poor woman out of the hallway with the help of the old housekeeper.

I was tempted to follow, but Holmes stayed put, studying the art, so I remained behind as well.

"Well, that was just—" I stopped, unable to think of a word that could collectively describe the chaotic assembly of feelings that setting foot in the Richardson house had stirred in me.

Holmes seemed to understand, for he nodded and said, "Indeed."

I cleared my throat, perhaps in an effort to clear my head. It didn't work even though Aurelia's cries had grown weak. Deciding to drown out her voice with my own, I said rather loudly, "I can't believe you managed to see the corners of her eyebrows."

Holmes looked pleased. "My vision is rather exceptional."

Rolling my eyes, I turned my attention to the wall and examined each work carefully. Most were portraits of ancestors who had passed away long ago. To break the monotony of these dark-suited men and exquisitely gowned women, a few dull paintings of landscapes had been systematically placed.

"I can see that the artwork is not to your liking, Watson," Holmes said, glancing at me.

"You know, if you had lived a few centuries ago, you would've been burned at the stake for witchcraft. Care to tell me how you knew that?"

"Simple. Your nose has a habit of flaring and the left part of your lips curls upwards when you disapprove of something." Somehow, over the course of our brief acquaintanceship, he had mastered every nuance of expression my face was capable of creating.

"Which painting do you think Aurelia was talking about?" I asked.

"Does it really matter? The unfortunate woman is mad as a hatter and should be institutionalized immediately." I was about to protest the rude choice of words, but just then, Holmes tilted his head towards the door the Richardsons had disappeared behind, from where an argument continued to ensue. "It appears the stepmother agrees with me."

"Stepmother? How did you know that?"

"Quite obvious, that. Aurelia and Mrs. Richardson share not an ounce of physical similarity, but what is more telling is her concern for the broken lamp. Ivory and metal matter to her more than flesh and bone." He craned his neck further, face scrunched in concentration. "She also considers Aurelia to be an embarrassment and doesn't want to invite her friends to the house because she thinks her stepdaughter may clobber them over the head." He turned to me with a look of disgust distorting his sharp features. "I can't listen to another word out of that vile woman's mouth. Come, Watson."

Before he could march down the hallway, however, I grabbed his arm. "Do you think *this* is the painting that upset Aurelia?"

I pointed at an oil on canvas, roughly eighty centimetres in length and considerably smaller than its neighbouring pieces. It featured a rugged landscape, lined with dark tree trunks and undergrowth beyond which one could see glimpses of a lake. I wouldn't have been surprised if the artist had captured a real place, somewhere up north, just on the brink of winter when the countryside became bleak and harsh. It was the only painting that featured woods, but I suddenly felt sheepish as Holmes shot a nonchalant glance at it.

"Broad brush strokes, an excessive amount of paint, and depressing colours — the work aptly captures a most hideous aspect of this country's landscape. I should not like to visit this place," Holmes said, completely ignoring my question. Before I could respond, he maneuvered me down the hallway, and we entered the kitchen, arm in arm.

The first person we saw was Mrs. Hudson. She was a plump woman with greying, frizzy hair that was habitually wound in a tight bun. Although she was about fifty-five years of age, it was difficult to tell by her smooth, chocolate-toned complexion and neat dress. The youthful effect was somewhat spoiled by the scowl that she usually wore, which was obviously the result of the hard labour imposed on her by the delinquent and awfully messy residents of Baker House. Being a naturally tidy person, I had never been chastised by her and, as a result, had not mingled with her much before this point. Today, surprisingly, she was smiling. In fact, she seemed to have forgotten the calamity from five minutes ago and relished the sight of us with a mischievous grin that I didn't quite understand. I shot an awkward glance in her direction and mustered a smile as she waved us over to the table where she was sitting.

"Oh, what a lovely pair you make! Sherlock, you didn't tell me you're seeing Ms. Watson."

"We're not dating," I said, immediately releasing myself from Holmes' hold. Unfortunately, my tempo and tone made me sound like an indignant child, and I blushed furiously.

Perhaps I had offended Holmes—that is, if he were capable of these kinds of sticky feelings— because this snappish retort followed: "Like many of today's youth, Mrs. H, I think Watson is presently exploring her sexuality. She spent all of September ogling that tall bloke who lives on our floor—captain of the football team, isn't he, Watson? I think she now fancies the brunette who works at the university bookstore. Hence, dating me is out of the question at this time."

Caught off-guard, I shot him a nasty glare, which he ignored as he propelled his slender body to join Mrs. Hudson. A rebuttal made my lips quiver, but for fear of sounding juvenile again, I put that and the overpowering heat in my cheeks aside and took in the splendour of my surroundings.

The kitchen was a shocking contrast to the dark wood panelling and Victorian theme of the rest of the house. It was the very picture of modernity, with its pearly white cabinets, radiant pendant lights, bar stools, and marble-topped counter space that looked as though it were seldom touched. A pair of rustic sliding doors dominated one wall while a row of large windows and a clear patio door made up most of the opposite wall. Near these windows sat a sleek, glass-topped dining table and chairs. Mrs. Hudson sat on one of these chairs; another was occupied by Aurelia Richardson, whose face was still wet with tears. Her agitation had ceased, however, and she stared absentmindedly through the patio door, which had been propped open with a rubber wedge. Her fingers twitched periodically, as though inclined to touch the glass. On the other side of this door stood the short and stocky form of the nurse, his neck flushed red. He was zealously puffing at a cigarette.

My gaze slid past him to the modestly sized, grassy yard that completed the rear of the Richardson home. I blinked in puzzlement, then squinted, wondering if my brain was distorting the scene before me.

There were holes everywhere, each accompanied by small mounds of dirt that lay in neat piles. Someone — a dirty child was what came to mind, although there appeared to be no such person in this household — had gone digging in the yard in a state of organized frenzy. My eyes slowly made their way to Aurelia.

"Aurelia loves to dig, don't you?" exclaimed a soft voice, no doubt in response to my look of surprise.

A blonde, wool-clad figure materialized next to Aurelia, holding a steaming mug of what smelled like cocoa. She was a rather petite woman, although the heavy, brown sweater, underneath which I spied multiple layers of clothing, gave her the comical appearance of a small head atop an oversized body. Admittedly, the air was cool inside the house, but I didn't understand why the woman had felt the need to wear thick joggers' pants and wool socks. She was no more than twenty-five years of age and very pretty. Yet her pale face, which looked as though it had been deprived of many nights' worth of sleep, seemed incredibly fatigued.

The mug was set in front of Aurelia, who, oblivious to the enticing smell of cocoa, glanced around the room. Her gaze finally fell on me and lingered as though hypnotically entranced. *Was there something on my face?* I wondered, fidgeting in my seat, and looked away.

The young woman with the thick sweater turned to us and introduced herself as Roksanda Dragomirov, the housekeeper. I was a bit taken aback by this; I had been expecting someone matronly like Mrs. Hudson. With a polite hello, I presented Holmes and myself as friends of Mrs. Hudson. Holmes offered no greeting but studied her with protuberant eyes, which eventually made poor Roksanda shuffle her feet awkwardly.

"Rokkie is the daughter of an old friend of mine," Mrs. Hudson said. "Thirty years ago, when Aurelia and her sister were little, Alistair needed far more hands to keep the house in order. I looked after the girls, and Rokkie's mother, bless her soul, took care of everything else. She's passed away now, but I look in on Rokkie from time to time. When she needed a job after graduation, I spoke to Alistair and got her hired."

Although she was smiling at Roksanda, her eyes looked sorrowful. This quickly transformed into astonishment — with a hint of indignation — when Holmes said, "Don't worry, Mrs. H, I am sure Miss Dragomirov will not waste away in housekeeping." The comment that followed almost immediately was meant to galvanize Roksanda: "Perhaps she can pursue her interest in the arts professionally."

Before the young housekeeper could speak, Mrs. Hudson interjected, "No, Rokkie, I didn't tell him a thing." She chuckled, having quickly forgiven Holmes for his earlier remark. "It's just what Sherlock does."

"Uh, okay," stammered Roksanda, examining Holmes with renewed interest. "I was an arts major, but nowadays it's hard to find time to even do a sketch. I still try though." Her large, amber eyes did an unhappy waltz around the kitchen. "How did you know I dabble in the arts?"

Holmes looked at her inquisitively, delaying his answer on purpose, but before he could launch into an explanation, I interrupted, "He saw the blue paint on your pinky."

Roksanda laughed sheepishly, holding up the paint-smeared finger I had noticed as she had given Aurelia the cocoa.

Holmes stared at me coldly. "Ultramarine, if I am not mistaken," he said, still frowning. "From the Latin *ultramarinus*, which means "beyond the sea". The name is an apt description since the pigment was imported to Europe from Afghanistan in the 14th and 15th centuries." The pedantic outburst spilled out almost too quickly for comprehension; Holmes was no doubt trying to recapture his audience, but they were otherwise occupied. Mrs. Hudson was now staring at me as though I were a prodigy, Roksanda was furiously rubbing the paint on her finger, and Aurelia — to my relief — watched the holes in the yard with longing, her cocoa still untouched. In typical Holmesian fashion, however, he directed everyone's attention back to him with the following enigmatic statement:

"Picking up artistic inclinations from a paint stain is not particularly clever, but what about a medical diagnosis based on the science of deduction? Now that would be clever, wouldn't you agree, Mrs. H?"

"It's more of an art than a science," I mumbled, but only Holmes heard my remark, and he chose to ignore it.

Much to his delight, Mrs. Hudson nodded enthusiastically. Then, she frowned. "Please don't say I have a brain tumour."

"Of course not, but your insomniac tendencies are aging you. It is true that insomnia increases with age — you have passed fifty now, eh, Mrs. H?" The answer to this was a glare, but Holmes continued, "The hormonal shifts you are encountering due to menopause are undoubtedly — " Again, another glare; this one managed to capture Holmes' attention, for he stopped to clear his throat loudly before saying, "Those bags underneath your eyes are starting to look permanent. Perhaps some eye cream? No? Anyway, I was referring to Miss Dra — ah, let us forgo formalities — Roksanda."

The housekeeper stiffened, no longer concerned by the paint that remained stuck to her finger. "What do you mean, Sherlock?"

"Holmes," came the correction automatically. "I prefer to be addressed by my surname. Only my mother called me Sher — " He stopped as was custom whenever he accidentally delved into any topic that was even remotely personal.

His reticence on the topic had convinced me that he had no family until a few days ago when he had offhandedly mentioned the existence of an older brother. No other details had been offered, however, and I had decided not to pry.

"If you can provide an explanation sometime today, that would be great," I said impatiently. "Roksanda is starting to look as though she might be sick." It seemed I wasn't the only person who was anxious to hear his deduction; even Aurelia had tuned into our conversation. Her eyes flitted back and forth between Holmes and the agitated housekeeper in a way that led me to suspect that she had been listening from the very beginning.

"Gladly," Holmes smirked. "The signs are quite easy to spot. I am not surprised that you haven't perceived them yourself due to your lack of medical knowledge—" I was an instant away from pointing out that a background in chemistry from a degree in progress hardly qualified as medical credentials when Holmes, perhaps sensing my rebuttal, carried on in haste, "Your fatigued face, sparse eyebrows, and cold intolerance are highly suggestive of hypothyroidism, Roksanda."

The hapless housekeeper, who looked as though she would rather be anywhere else on the planet than here, involuntarily fingered an eyebrow. Her hand shot down almost immediately, and her face reddened. Holmes, unfortunately, was impervious to her embarrassment.

"If you will allow me," he said, "I can gently press the outside of your throat to see if there is any swelling in your thyroid, which can help confirm my diagnosis." His face twitched with an excited curiosity that bordered on fanaticism, which, along with his outstretched hand, was probably what propelled Roksanda to step back, looking faint-hearted.

I intervened to rescue the poor damsel once again. "You'll go see a real doctor, won't you, Roksanda?" The answer to this was profuse nodding on the part of Roksanda. "If you're done harassing people, Holmes, maybe we can talk about something pleasant."

"Pleasantry didn't bring us here," Holmes murmured darkly, casting a sideways glance at Aurelia, who had returned her attention to the yard. Mrs. Hudson seemed to understand his subtle command.

"Aurelia, why don't you take advantage of the sunny weather and carry on with your excavations?" she asked, her voice soft and slow as though she were talking to a child.

"But it's chilly," Roksanda protested. "What if she catches a cold? Mr. Richardson won't—"

But Aurelia stood, put on the thick sweater that hung from her chair, and dragged her slippered feet to the patio door. To our surprise, she paused there and turned to look at Holmes, who was watching her movements with unblinking eyes.

"Is that a pocket watch?" she asked quietly, motioning at the protrusion in Holmes' breast pocket.

Wearing an expression of surprise mingled with something else, Holmes pulled out the gold pocket watch I had seen him consult for the time on one or two occasions. Although it looked more appropriate in the dainty hands of someone from a century ago, he preferred it to pulling out his phone. Unfortunately, this had not escaped the notice of Baker House's rowdy bunch, and after a rather nasty incident involving the pocket watch being thrown out a window, Holmes had opted to using a watch of the wrist-worn variety. I was relieved to see that it had survived the fall, although the exterior looked quite bruised.

Holmes held out the pocket watch for all to see, which automatically prompted us to inch closer. Aurelia, however, remained rooted to the spot, but her head shot forward and her eyes bulged with curiosity.

"One of my graduate students had one like that," she murmured. "Hers was decorated with rubies and sapphires. Fake, of course, but beautiful nonetheless since it was a gift from her lover. Such a smart girl, yes, she was. So much potential."

It was the most the woman had said in our presence up to that point, and the coherence and clarity of her speech baffled even Holmes. Discourse from Aurelia though was as rare as it was short because her lips clamped shut shortly thereafter, and she marched out the door with Mrs. Hudson trailing her. I watched as she stationed herself next to a small mound of dirt by the stone wall that gated the property. Her vacant expression lifted once again, and a feverish energy overtook her as she began her "excavations".

Chapter 4 A Conversation with the Housekeepers

"Finally, having drawn every other cover and picked up no scent, I tried my luck with the housekeeper."

—Sir Arthur Conan Doyle, *The Adventure of the Norwood Builder*

"Mrs. Richardson just hates the state the yard's in," Roksanda said, peering through the patio door after Mrs. Hudson returned.

"Humph," Mrs. Hudson snorted. "The first Mrs. Richardson was a fine lady, but this Portia Richardson—argh. I think old age has muddled Alistair's taste in women." Still scowling, she turned her attention to Holmes and me. "What do you make of the case so far?"

"The case?" Roksanda interjected, joining us at the table. "You were being serious when you said you were bringing people to investigate?" She gawked at us with skepticism, just like Mr.

53

Richardson had. It was apparent from her expression that she thought us too young to play detective, and I wholeheartedly agreed.

"I didn't tell you because I know where you stand on this matter, but before we try and persuade Alistair to institutionalize Aurelia, we need to make sure nothing fishy is going on."

"Fishy? There's nothing fishy going on. That poor woman is sick. She needs—"

"Roksanda!" Mrs. Hudson's face, which looked severe at first but quickly disintegrated into despair, silenced the young woman. "I helped raise her. I can't bear to see her like this." Her voice quivered. "If something is going on here, if something is preventing Aurelia from recovering—" She turned abruptly to Holmes, eyes tearful.

Holmes' reaction was mild discomfort at the sight of an emotional Mrs. Hudson, but he regained his composure quickly. "You two seem to be at odds with what is happening to Dr. Richardson. Kindly start from the beginning, Mrs. H, and omit no detail."

I could tell that Roksanda had been on the verge of saying something in response to Mrs. Hudson, but there was a commanding quality to Holmes' voice that, based on his preference, persuaded people to either talk or be silent. In this case, Mrs. Hudson spoke and Roksanda closed her mouth, and Holmes leaned forward and nestled his chin onto his clasped fingers. His eyes closed and his face became the embodiment of grim concentration.

"I believe Aurelia's troubles started about six years ago," Mrs. Hudson began. "It was long after my time as housekeeper and before I got Roksanda this job, so the details are sparse. Alistair has been very close-lipped about his daughter's condition, even to me. He's very protective of her, so we don't really know the beginning of the story.

"All I know is that Aurelia was on an archaeological expedition in some remote corner of the world, an island somewhere, when she had a breakdown. She was institutionalized for a few years. Finally, in January, Alistair convinced the doctors to let her come home. He hired Alejo to look after her, and everything was fine. I visited her often during this time. She was doing so well."

Here, Roksanda looked as though she were bursting to say something, but one stern look from Mrs. Hudson made her rethink an interruption.

"So what happened?" I asked.

Mrs. Hudson became mournful. "I don't know. Summer passed, fall arrived, and Aurelia changed. She was always terrified; she was nervous and jumpy, and she began seeing things."

"She became hysterical," Roksanda added. "The doctors increased her medication because Mr. Richardson refused to send her back to the hospital. That didn't do much. She's been getting worse ever since."

Holmes opened his eyes. "Was today the first time she tried to take her life?" he inquired. It was clear that Roksanda had been made aware of the incident with the rope since there was dismay rather than shock or surprise on her face. Mrs. Hudson became tearful again, and her lips pressed into a sniffle as the young housekeeper resumed the tale.

"The first attempt happened a few days ago," she said. "That morning, Aurelia became frantic because she thought someone was chasing her. She ran out of the house and straight into traffic. The streets are normally very quiet, but in the mornings, cars tend to cut through the neighbourhood to get to the main road, and one almost ran her down. If the driver hadn't managed to slam his breaks..." Roksanda drew a shaky breath. "I still remember the way Mr. Richardson looked as Alejo carried Aurelia back into the house, as though his worst fear had been realized. He knew Aurelia was going to get hurt if she stayed in this house, but he still didn't do anything about it. That's when I approached Martha. Something had to be done."

How strange, I thought. From my brief encounter with Mr. Richardson, the only faults I could see with his character were his gruff manner and insuppressible anger, although in his defence, Aurelia's safety, or lack of it, had instigated both. I could excuse and understand his behaviour towards the nurse. What surprised me was his insistence on keeping his daughter home. Did the idea of institutionalizing Aurelia torture him as much as he claimed, or was there another reason behind his adamant refusal?

"Do you have any theories that may explain Dr. Richardson's behaviour change, Mrs. H?" Holmes asked.

"I—" began Mrs. Hudson. "Look, I know you modern folk don't have a place in your mind for anything that—that—"

"Defies science?" I suggested helpfully.

Before Mrs. Hudson could reply, Holmes cut in, "Are you saying that a supernatural element is hindering Dr. Richardson's recovery?" The sneering skepticism was painfully noticeable in his tone.

Mrs. Hudson's response, I was pleased to see, was a defiant stare. "I know you of all people wouldn't be open to such an idea, but I think it deserves investigation, so investigate." It was a command, and Holmes' smirk faded under the woman's watch. She continued, "Aurelia didn't just go from being fine to delusional overnight. I just feel—"

"Intuition will only get us so far. I need facts," Holmes interrupted. "To point out the obvious, Dr. Richardson hasn't been in good form for a long time. Psychotic relapse is not unheard of, even if one has the good fortune of having a wealthy father and excellent medical care."

Mrs. Hudson sighed. "I think something is terrifying Aurelia, and I'm not sure it's all in her head. Take the rope, for instance. I've never seen a rope around the house before."

"Um, Martha, you don't work here anymore," Roksanda said, although her tone remained deferential. "Lots of things have changed. That rope could've easily come from the shed where all the gardening tools are."

"Have you seen a rope in the shed?" Mrs. Hudson asked pointedly.

"Well, no, but I'm fairly sure a ghost didn't poof it into existence and hand it to Aurelia."

"I am inclined to agree with Roksanda," Holmes said. "But I will humour you for just a moment, Mrs. H. Tell me, is this house haunted?"

Mrs. Hudson's mouth opened, then closed almost instantly. Roksanda butted in, "The house is definitely not haunted."

"So perhaps the ghost has latched itself onto Dr. Richardson? Perhaps it whispers into her ear —"

"Stop it, Sherlock!" Mrs. Hudson bellowed. "I know when I'm being mocked. To answer your question seriously, I haven't noticed anything strange in the house during my visits, and it's certainly possible the ghost is attached only to Aurelia." Somehow, she was permitted to say "Sherlock".

I could tell that Mrs. Hudson's resolute answer irked Holmes, but he assumed a tolerant smile and said, "Is there a reason a ghost would specifically target Dr. Richardson? Has she angered the spirit world in any way?"

Despite the smile, all I heard was derisive heckling. Judging by the hint of anger that remained in her voice, it seemed Mrs. Hudson had noticed this as well. "Isn't it obvious? She's the weakest one here. Demons always attach themselves to—"

"Ah, yes, the weakest link…Human agents have a tendency to do that too, Mrs. H," Holmes said. "Perhaps the approach of Halloween is obumbrating your sense and reasoning. Don't you think it is more reasonable to assume that someone brought the rope into the house? Or perhaps Dr. Richardson had a hand in procuring it after all."

But the old housekeeper shook her head. "No, that doesn't make sense. Where on earth would Aurelia go to find a rope? And I refuse to believe that anyone in this household would harm her." The adamancy in her voice nearly compelled me to believe her, but then I remembered Portia Richardson's look of disdain at the sight of her panic-stricken stepdaughter. Was she callous enough to coax Aurelia into taking her own life?

Apparently, Holmes had similar thoughts. He glanced in the direction of the hallway where we had encountered Mrs. Richardson, and then conducted a careful examination of Roksanda, before speaking. "Do tell us what is on your mind, Roksanda. You, like I, but unlike Watson and Mrs. H, seem to believe that human hands are involved. Whom do you suspect?"

Before I could state, as convincingly as I could, that I didn't believe in ghosts, Roksanda jumped in, eager to respond. Her tone, however, was hesitant since Mrs. Hudson was glaring at her.

"Uh, well—" she began. "Personally, I don't think anything weird is going on. Aurelia likes to wander, and she has the freedom to do so without restrictions because Alejo isn't as attentive as he should be. She could've easily come across the rope somewhere in the house, or maybe she took it from the neighbour's backyard. They're never home anyway. She could've wandered over there in the middle of the night, and no one would ever know." She paused. "Look, Aurelia is very sick and needs proper care—care she isn't getting in this house. I don't know if Mr. Richardson really is heartbroken over this, or maybe he's too embarrassed to tell people where his daughter is if she gets institutionalized again—"

"Aurelia is not an embarrassment to Alistair," Mrs. Hudson said sharply.

"Fine, even if that's not the case, Aurelia is still not getting the care she needs by staying here." Roksanda frowned, her gaze extending past the patio door to where Alejo stood, lighting what appeared to his second, or perhaps third, cigarette. Beyond him, Aurelia was squatting on the ground, carefully shovelling dirt with a bright red sand shovel that would have looked more appropriate in the hands of a child in a sandbox.

"You don't think Alejo is adequate help?" Holmes inquired.

"He's all muscle and no brains," Roksanda said, dropping her voice to a whisper in case the nurse could hear us through the open door, although he seemed oblivious to our conversation. "Apart from all the smoke breaks, it would be nice if he responds once in a while."

"What do you mean?" I asked.

Roksanda's frown deepened. "Well, whenever Aurelia wanders and gets herself into trouble, we have to practically yell to grab Alejo's attention. Sometimes, he could be standing right in front of me, but he doesn't respond. The man is lost inside his own head, or he's turning deaf. How can we rely on him to take care of Aurelia?"

Holmes looked vaguely amused by this. He stroked his chin thoughtfully and then, without warning, called out to the nurse. I knew his voice would have carried over clearly to where Alejo was standing, and yet there was no response. I heard Holmes murmur something that sounded like "how interesting" before he resorted to hollering the man's name.

Alejo spun around as though he had been electrocuted, which had no doubt been Holmes' objective. As I peered down the hallway for signs of a startled Mr. and Mrs. Richardson,

Holmes motioned the nurse inside, a command that was obeyed with equal parts hesitation and discomfort. Failing to squeeze his bulk through the partially open door, Alejo unintentionally knocked aside the door wedge, causing the door to bang shut behind him. We all jumped, but the nurse's antsiness persisted long after we had recovered. I wondered if he had overheard our conversation after all, but if he had, he didn't acknowledge it verbally. In all likelihood, it was Holmes' unblinking scrutiny that was unnerving the man.

"Alejo," Holmes said with what he thought was an encouraging smile but was in actuality the probing expression of an unhinged scientist dissecting a specimen. "How many packs of cigarettes do you smoke daily?"

The nurse's mouth hung open in surprise for a moment. He glanced at Mrs. Hudson, who gave him a reassuring nod. His bulk appeared to deflate a bit when he let out a breath and said timidly, "I don't smoke a lot, only when I'm stressed." He seemed to want to add to this, perhaps a statement about how his stress levels had peaked after starting his present position. There was little time for such elaborations, however, since Holmes went on with his interrogation without pause.

"Excellent. Next question: have any of your previous occupations involved a noisy work environment?"

The nurse's bafflement grew—as it did for the rest of us—as he stuttered a weak "no".

"Is there even the remotest possibility that you are experiencing hearing loss despite your youth?"

"Uh, no."

I thought the response sounded more like a question, but Holmes seemed satisfied. "Very good," he said. "Now tell me, what is your full name?"

Alejo's demeanor reverted to discomfort, but this time he eyeballed the rest of us suspiciously. We peered back with innocent expressions; we were as perplexed with Holmes' line of questioning as he was.

"Alejo S-Santos."

"Ah! That sounds vaguely familiar. Give me one moment, please."

Holmes recollected his thoughts in silence for the most part, although once he mumbled out loud what sounded a lot like "war". Watching him, Alejo fidgeted in agitation. Unlike Mrs. Hudson and Roksanda, he was far from amused by Holmes' eccentricity. For some strange reason, the interrogation was distressing him.

"I've got it! Alejo Santos—a decorated Filipino World War II soldier, who then turned to politics—"

"Holmes, it's clear Alejo's parents were fans of this man and named their son after him," I said, and the nurse gave a confirmatory nod. "Is there a point to your sermon?" I had to interrupt since no one else would; Roksanda and Alejo were too polite to do so, and Mrs. Hudson seemed to enjoy listening to Holmes talk.

"There is always a point, Watson," Holmes replied sharply. "You may return to your post, Alejo."

The nurse scurried away, closing the patio door as he exited the room. Perhaps this was his way of putting up a solid barrier between himself and us, specifically Holmes. I could see him shakily light another cigarette. The stench of the ones he had already smoked lingered in the kitchen.

"What was all that about?" Mrs. Hudson and I asked in unison. I was grateful for the extra voice since Holmes had a habit of addressing my questions only when it was convenient for him to do so, which was usually sometime after my initial burst of curiosity. If I had perfected any of my virtues during my six weeks' worth of interactions with him, it was patience. Luckily, I didn't need to wait in this case; Holmes didn't dare wave away a question from the austere Mrs. Hudson.

"That young man is not going deaf," he began, motioning at the smoking nurse.

I found it comical that Holmes habitually referred to people as though he were decades older; it was especially entertaining in this case since he was far younger than Alejo and half the man's size. Too curious to hear what he had to say, I decided not to taunt him.

"There is some agreement in the scientific community that a connection exists between smoking and hearing loss, but Alejo reported that he is not a frequent smoker. Can you confirm that, Roksanda?"

"Yeah, I guess he doesn't smoke that much — at least, he didn't during the summer," the housekeeper replied almost grudgingly. "But you know how it is. Everything is done by the book when starting a job. Then, people get comfortable and start slacking."

For me, however, it was easier to believe that Aurelia's disintegrating mental state had sent the nurse spiralling into the smoky arms of nicotine. Perhaps it was the upright way he held himself or his forever-serious face — he just didn't seem like the type who would take his duties lightly. My conviction, however, wavered almost immediately as I recalled something that hadn't occurred to me before.

"I thought as much due to the lack of physical traits typical of heavy smokers," Holmes said, interrupting my thoughts. "Onto the next point then: noise. The literature is filled with studies on noise-induced hearing loss. Take, for instance, an Indonesian study that was published last year on workers at a palm oil factory —" Having caught my scowl, he stopped. "Hence my question on noisy work environments. Considering Alejo's line of work, I reckoned he would respond in the negative, which he did." A quick breath punctuated his flow and then he continued, "Although there is an abundance of maladies that may induce hearing loss and not be physically obvious, even to highly observant persons like me," — I couldn't help but roll my eyes, even though the statement wasn't an exaggeration — "I am inclined to believe that Alejo can hear just as well as you or I." He paused. "Well, perhaps not as well as me."

"So why doesn't he always respond when we call him?" Roksanda asked.

"Perhaps he is just spaced out, as you have already suggested. Maybe he doesn't like you and purposely ignores you. Maybe he likes you and you make him nervous, so he pretends he doesn't hear you," Holmes responded, a slight smile curving his thin lips. "Or maybe there is something more to this little problem."

But he didn't elaborate on this and changed the topic. "Alejo isn't the only source of — uh — disturbance in this house. Roksanda, please share what you wanted to reveal on several prior occasions during this conversation but chose not to, perhaps owing to the fact that Mrs. H intimidates you. We both know she is a dear."

Mrs. Hudson looked both charmed and indignant — if it were possible for a face to capture such contradictory expressions. She remained silent though, which perhaps motivated Roksanda to disclose a few more secrets about the Richardsons.

"Well, the missing—" she began, but we didn't find out what had gone missing.

The arrival of a stranger halted our conversation.

Chapter 5 Buried or Taken?

"You will remember, Lestrade, the sensation caused by the disappearance of this valuable jewel and the vain efforts of the London police to recover it."

—Sir Arthur Conan Doyle, *The Adventure of the Six Napoleons*

THE SMELL OF STRONG PERFUME DRIFTED UP MY nostrils a few seconds before the woman marched into the kitchen, bringing with her a flurry of motions and a cacophony of sounds. The click-clack of her stilettos, the swish of her costly fur collar coat, and the masses of shopping bags, each decorated with the logo of some posh boutique I could only window shop at, captured the attention of every person in the room. She was also very pregnant.

"The sister," Holmes muttered.

Instantly, I saw the resemblance between this woman and Aurelia, despite the carrot-coloured

68

hair, pink cheeks, and bright red lips. Both sisters possessed the same deep brown eyes, aristocratic nose, and small frame. Whereas Aurelia was devoid of colour, this woman shone exuberantly, partly due to the heavy makeup and perhaps the pregnancy, and partly because of the loud voice that emerged when she noticed Holmes and me.

"Oh! We have visitors! Martha! I didn't know you were coming by today. It's so good to see you."

Mrs. Hudson was the only person who seemed happy to see her. Roksanda had turned away, suddenly preoccupied by either Alejo, who was now ejecting streams of smoke through his nostrils, or the yard beyond (it was difficult to tell where she was looking). Holmes was studying the newcomer in his usual hawkish manner, and I shifted uncomfortably in my paint-stained overalls. As soon as the woman had dumped her purchases on the kitchen counter and waltzed over to where we sat, Mrs. Hudson eagerly presented her as Aurora Giordano, Aurelia's younger sister. Holmes and I introduced ourselves. Aurora offered me a polite nod and eyed my overalls in what she thought was an indiscreet manner. Holmes, on the other hand, received a rather sweet smile as she took a seat next to him.

Although I was an exception, women in general were often taken in by Holmes' lean form and contrasting pale face and dark hair.

For instance, nearly half the ladies (and two guys) at Baker House had eyed him with interest at some point in the past six weeks. It was usually after he opened his mouth that they fled, unless he was being charming on purpose, which had happened once in my presence when he had managed to convince the RA not to report his habit of smoking in his room. She had left the room looking rather spellbound, and sure enough, no word of his delinquency had ever reached the university.

"Tell me all about your day, Aurora," Mrs. Hudson said, apparently having forgotten our more important discussion from only moments before.

Aurora obliged only too willingly, and we were painfully subjected to a monologue about a shopping expedition to "grab a few essentials" and lunch at an all-you-can-eat sushi bar with her girlfriends. She finished by complaining about the chill outside.

"Half an hour warming up in the sauna will do me good," she exclaimed, standing up.

Holmes mumbled something and stared at the woman's belly long enough to stir feelings of awkwardness in all of us. My cheeks began to redden in embarrassment as Aurora glared first at Holmes, and then at Mrs. Hudson, her face silently asking for an explanation. Mrs. Hudson shrugged and Aurora placed her hands protectively over her tummy.

"Uh, Holmes?" I called out.

My summons managed to bring him out of his entranced state, but he ignored me and said to Aurora, "You are nearly at term. When are you due?"

"Soon." A sour expression accompanied the cold response.

I had a feeling she was being vague on purpose and was eager to quit the conversation and the room, her pleasant first impression of Holmes having disintegrated. Holmes, however, had plans that opposed hers.

"Please do stay, Aurora. We have much to discuss. Mrs. H, you should tell her why Watson and I are here."

Just as she had broken the news to Roksanda, Mrs. Hudson tactfully explained everything, including the incident with Aurelia and the rope. Aurora was silent for a minute afterwards. Her face had transformed from its debonair demeanour to something darker and more serious. She glanced at the yard where Aurelia, body partly obscured by a growing mound of dirt, could be seen methodically stroking something with a large paint brush. Then, she glanced at Holmes and me, and her belittling expression mirrored the one her father had worn. Mrs. Hudson took her hand and gave it a squeeze, and Aurora sighed and sat back down.

"My sister isn't well," she finally said. "But we're taking care of her here. I don't want to see her institutionalized again."

Although nobody else had noticed, I saw Roksanda roll her eyes and look distastefully at the shopping bags that littered the counter. She seemed to want to say something that I wagered would stir up an argument, but by the time she spoke her face had assumed a neutral air.

"We were discussing the missing jewellery when you walked in," she said.

My interest peaked hearing this. There was something thrilling about missing valuables. With far too much enthusiasm, I asked, "Misplaced or stolen?"

Mrs. Hudson huffed. "There's certainly no thief here."

"I overheard Mrs. Richardson complaining yesterday morning that her diamond bracelet is missing," Roksanda said.

"That dunce of a woman probably put it somewhere and forgot all about it," Mrs. Hudson snapped, then said to Aurora, "No offence."

"I've come to tolerate her, Martha, but that's about it. She's not family, not really," Aurora answered.

"If I may interrupt," Holmes started, "Watson and I are in the dark here. If someone would be kind enough to tell the story from the beginning, rather than shout obscure details from the middle, we would appreciate it. Although I can easily infer the details, for Watson's benefit, one of you should tell the tale."

I had little time to unbottle my livid reaction because Mrs. Hudson interjected, "There's no mystery here, Sherlock. Aurelia took Portia's jewellery. Some of it has already been recovered."

"Only one actually," Roksanda chipped in. "A bracelet, but I'm not sure Aurelia did it."

Two voices spoke out simultaneously. From what I could tell, Mrs. Hudson said something along the lines of: "It was obviously Aurelia, but she didn't know what she was doing!" Holmes' remark was nearly swallowed by Mrs. Hudson's furious one, but I was fairly certain he muttered, "And the plot thickens! The housekeeper-turned-detective has a fresh perspective to offer. How exciting!" If this had been laced with sarcasm, I couldn't tell. Roksanda hadn't heard his description of her; her attention was occupied solely by the protesting Mrs. Hudson.

"We'd better start from the beginning like Sher—uh—Holmes suggested," she said. She was clearly having trouble referring to Holmes by his preferred way of being addressed; it had taken me a while to get used to as well.

Mrs. Hudson's eye twitched and her mouth was on the verge of more protestations, but Roksanda launched into the tale I had been waiting atiptoe to hear.

"A few months ago, one of Mrs. Richardson's rings went missing," she began. "Mr. Richardson dismissed it, thinking she misplaced it, but it never turned up. A couple of weeks later, another ring went missing. Mrs. Richardson went ballistic. She practically accused everyone in the house—didn't even spare Aurelia. Mr. Richardson had to bribe her with a trip to some fashion expo in Milan to calm her down. They're supposed to leave for that tonight." It was apparent that she wanted to add a note of relief, but common courtesy for her employers stopped her. "A few weeks after the ring, a bracelet was taken."

"Were the robberies reported to the police?" I asked.

"Theft, Watson," Holmes interrupted.

I shrugged. "It's the same thing."

"It is *not*," he said. "Robbery is more violent, involving coercion or force, for example, use of a weapon. Theft refers simply to intentionally taking something that belongs to someone else. Hence, *theft* is the correct term in this scenario." He turned to Roksanda. "Please go on."

And the housekeeper started talking again. "The security system didn't go off, so the thief didn't come from outside. Mr. Richardson didn't want to involve the police. It was a family matter, he said, and he's very protective of the family, which is why I'm surprised he allowed you guys to—uh—investigate. Anyway, one day, we were sitting right here for lunch when we saw—"

"'We' refers to whom?" Holmes asked.

"I remember that day very well," Aurora interjected just as the housekeeper opened her mouth to reply. "It was me, dad, and Aurelia, and Roksanda was serving lunch."

"And where was Mrs. Richardson?"

"Probably at the country club. She spends more time there than here anyway."

"Ah, I see. So you were all here, having a pleasant family lunch, adoring the view of the yard. Perhaps someone caught a glint of something shiny in the dirt?"

Aurora nodded, awe-struck.

"Nice way to spoil the ending," I muttered, to which Holmes mumbled what sounded like "painfully obvious" and "apparent even to a child". To Aurora, he asked in more audible tones who had spotted the glint.

"Dad," she recalled. "We went over to investigate, and sure enough, in one of the dirt mounds, half buried, was the bracelet."

"And Dr. Richardson confessed to taking it?" Holmes asked.

"Well, no, she denied it. She actually got really upset seeing the bracelet and went to her room without finishing her lunch."

"You say she became upset seeing the bracelet, rather than when she was accused of taking it?"

"Of course, she was upset seeing the bracelet," Aurora said. "Its discovery meant that it would be taken away from her. The poor thing had probably envisioned some grand unveiling during one of her excavations."

"I highly doubt that," Holmes murmured, then said out loud, "I assume none of your jewellery was touched?" Aurora nodded, and he continued, "Now, describe the two rings and the bracelet to me."

"Uh, both were gold diamond rings, I think. The bracelet was rose gold with alternating rubies and sapphires."

Holmes' eyes lit up. "Ah! I can see why Dr. Richardson would take the bracelet, but why the rings?"

Roksanda, who had been quietly watching the exchange between Holmes and Aurora, now said, "What do you mean by that?"

"Dr. Richardson has a special interest in rubies and sapphires. I believe she mentioned that right before she left for the yard."

"She did?" we exclaimed in unison.

"Her graduate student had a pocket watch adorned with these gemstones."

"And that prompted her to steal her stepmother's bracelet?" I asked skeptically. "That makes no sense."

Again, Holmes' voice became a low murmur. "No, it doesn't." His gaze extended beyond the window and landed on the distant figure of Aurelia. His face, I noted, wore an indecipherable expression. On the contrary, Mrs. Hudson's irritation was plain for all to see—and hear.

"It goes without saying," she began, "that the other pieces are buried somewhere in the yard.

It's just a matter of finding them, so there's no thief — only a troubled mind."

Holmes looked at her thoughtfully. "Do you think Mr. Richardson would mind if I tested your theory with my metal detector?"

"You have a metal detector?" I asked, smirking.

"Oh, yes. Have you never noticed it in my room? No? Well, I am not surprised."

I could have recited a monologue on the hodgepodge state of Holmes' room and the medley of papers, books, and trinkets he took comfort in surrounding himself with, but I opted for a condensed complaint: "Things are usually much more noticeable when there's less clutter."

Holmes frowned. "I have a great many possessions and only a minuscule room to call home in this country."

Although his unhappy expression was transitory, it made me wonder if he were homesick. I made a mental note to be nicer to him but instantly forgot when he resumed badgering Mrs. Hudson about the metal detector. To my surprise, she seemed hesitant. In fact, no amount of pleading on Holmes' part persuaded her. Was she afraid that the rest of the missing jewellery wouldn't be found in the yard? If Holmes' recovery efforts were to fail, would that suggest there was a thief in the house? My naturally suspicious mind made a daring leap — perhaps Mrs. Hudson knew the jewellery wouldn't be found in the yard. I tried to picture her portly form prowling about the house in the middle of the night, fingers at the ready to pocket all that was valuable. Try as I might, this was incredibly hard to imagine. It was easier to envision Aurelia absentmindedly collecting the valuables for some arcane purpose and burying them with ritualistic ardour.

This thought prompted another more controversial one. My eyes automatically travelled to Aurelia's distant form. I was tempted to voice it, but doing so in front of Mrs. Hudson and Aurora, both of whom seemed very protective of Aurelia, required audacity, which Holmes possessed in abundance, but I had little of.

"Ah, Watson, what a conspiratorial suspicion!" Holmes exclaimed, startling me. I flinched. In his usual ghostly manner, he had read my thoughts, although if prompted, he would deny being psychic and would explain how he had used subtle facial queues and other hogwash to deduce my thoughts. He had done this multiple times since our inaugural rendezvous; the first demonstration had awoken a renewed belief in clairvoyance, the second time had inspired awe, and every instance afterwards had been outright irritating.

"Well, go on and expose me," I grumbled, bracing myself.

"I will, but first a few questions for Aurora." He cleared his throat dramatically. "Does Alejo supervise Aurelia as she takes her medication? That is, does he watch her as she puts her pills in her mouth and swallows?"

"Uh, yes, I think so," Aurora replied, raising an eyebrow.

"Excellent. Has Aurelia ever pursued acting lessons?"

"No, not that I know of. Why on earth would you ask such a question!"

Holmes ignored this. "Would you say she is a natural then? How would you rate her ability to be theatrical, say on a scale of one to ten, ten being outstanding?"

The sound that escaped Aurora's lips resembled something feral. This may have been why Holmes went on to the next question without waiting for a response. "How often does Aurelia leave the house?"

"She doesn't like going outside; it overwhelms her sometimes. But she takes walks in the park that's on the other side of our backyard with Alejo every couple of days— dad's orders."

Now Holmes roped Roksanda into the conversation. "I presume you are both around Aurelia a lot, so you are the best candidates to answer my next question, but even then, I am not certain your answer will be correct." Both women pressed forward—Aurora, bemused and suspicious, and Roksanda, visibly excited. "Is there a possibility that Aurelia is not as ill as she appears to be? Is she perhaps taking the jewellery intentionally?"

Aurora's chair made a horrible scraping sound as it was flung backwards. She stood up angrily. "My sister is sick. She's not a thief. Don't you dare come into our home and throw around accusations!"

"It was a question, not an accusation. Not yet anyway," Holmes grunted. "It is not good form to accuse before observation and deduction." His expression as he watched Aurora was one I could neither describe nor explain, but it made her nervous enough to take a small step back. She looked furiously at Mrs. Hudson, who shrugged helplessly. There was no doubt that Aurora would pester the older woman into dismissing us. She would seek this permission out of respect, of course; in reality, it didn't matter what Mrs. Hudson said. I knew my hours inside this captivating house were limited, and it was all Holmes' fault. Unfortunately, he hadn't finished aggravating Aurora.

"So, tell me, why does a wealthy, married woman in her mid-thirties move back home?" he drawled.

Aurora reddened. "Late twenties," she corrected through gritted teeth. Her actual answer, which I was sure would never come anyway, was interrupted by the shriek of what sounded like a terrified animal. We all jumped, the imperturbable Holmes included.

Chapter 6 Aurelia's Discovery

"Very curious, and the story that hangs round it will strike you as being more curious still."

—Sir Arthur Conan Doyle, *The Musgrave Ritual*

IT WAS NO ORDINARY HORROR-MOVIE SCREAM though. It sounded repeatedly, almost like an alarm, and with every scream, the terror in Aurelia's voice grew. Of course, I knew the damsel in distress was Aurelia; the wailing had rung clearly from the direction of the yard. I could see her scrambling to her feet, her petite figure blurring as she raced across the yard, tripped over a mound of earth, and fell flat on her face.

Mrs. Hudson, Holmes, and I sprang to our feet, but Roksanda was already at the door. "Stay here," she ordered. "Too many people will only upset her more." She practically flew into the yard, leaving the door to bang shut behind

81

her, and ran after Alejo, who was already making his way towards Aurelia's fallen form. Unlike the nurse and the housekeeper, Aurora hadn't moved. Instead, her face had contorted into a look of fierce irritation.

"I can't deal with one of her episodes right now," she muttered, slumping back into her chair. It was shocking to see how abruptly her expression of indignation and sisterly concern had changed into annoyance.

I craned my neck to see what was happening in the yard. Roksanda and Alejo were bent over Aurelia, who appeared to be lying in a fetal position, although my view was partially obstructed by the elevated deck and several mounds of dirt in the vicinity. The two continued to prod the woman for another minute, and perhaps they had finally compelled her to speak because Roksanda straightened suddenly and jogged over to the spot Aurelia had been carrying out her excavations just moments before. She started looking around, jabbing at the dirt with her socked foot.

"Do you think we should—" I began.

"Yes, we should," Holmes responded, and then strutted out the door. Mrs. Hudson and I were quick to follow. Aurora didn't budge from her chair.

Much to our surprise, Holmes began walking towards Roksanda. I yanked his arm and hissed, "Why are you going that way? We need to make sure Aurelia is okay." He didn't look happy about changing course but followed silently as Mrs. Hudson and I led the way in the opposite direction. The site that lay before us nearly made me gasp.

Confusion, shock, and sheer, dreadful panic—these were the words that came to mind when I saw Aurelia, but words could barely describe the intense emotion that emanated from the poor woman. Like a fearful animal, she lay on her side, body scrunched up protectively and eyes closed, with one hand hiding half of her tear-stained face while the other rhythmically struck the ground. The shrieks had died away; she was crying softly now. Despite our inquiries, she neither looked at us nor spoke a word. Seeing her in such a state, weeping like a pitiful child, nearly made my eyes water, but I shook away the feeling and tried to imitate Holmes, who stared stoically at the scene before us. Mrs. Hudson, on the other hand, was overcome with emotion. She knelt, took Aurelia's head into her lap, and patted her hair with a grandmotherly gentleness.

I had no idea what had upset the poor woman. The yard was a mess. Disrupted patches of grass and fresh dirt littered the place, but I noticed, upon closer inspection, that there was a level of organization to the woman's "excavations". Some of the holes contained random household objects, which I doubted Aurelia had found buried in the yard. The Richardson family had clearly gone along with her digging games, or Aurelia had placed the items there herself to add authenticity to her excavations. I glanced back to where Roksanda was; had Aurelia found something there that had upset her? From my vantage point, I could see only disrupted earth, but it seemed Roksanda had found nothing of interest. She was still poking at the dirt with her foot. I could spot nothing in the yard capable of triggering Aurelia's panicked outburst.

"I agree completely," Holmes murmured in my ear. "Perhaps it was a tarantula that has already fled the scene, or maybe there is another explanation."

Luckily, there was no sign of a scuttling arachnid, but I also didn't see any evidence of Holmes' "another explanation". Perhaps he had said that just to rouse my curiosity in the hopes that I would become desperate enough to plead for an answer. I decided not to give him the satisfaction as punishment for having read my thoughts again.

Roksanda approached us, looking grim. Silently, she motioned Alejo towards the patio door, which prompted him to try to prop Aurelia into a standing position. She refused to move or be moved, however. As this struggle ensued, I leaned over to the housekeeper and murmured, "What happened?"

"Body parts," was her startling, whispered response.

Naturally, Holmes overheard this, but unlike me, it didn't mute him into a stunned silence. He knelt and gingerly pushed aside a thick strand of hair from Aurelia's face. He then pried away the hand that covered the rest of her face. Aurelia stared up at him in alarm.

"What did you see, Dr. Richardson?" he asked, his voice at the softest I had ever heard it.

The poor woman sat up but gripped Mrs. Hudson's hand tightly. She stared straight ahead, but I had a feeling she was using every ounce of her mental strength to resist looking at the excavation site she had run away from. There was fear in her eyes and it was genuine. I immediately felt guilty for suspecting her of being a good actress and thief.

"She said there were body parts buried in the ground," Roksanda told us. "But there's nothing there."

This declaration pushed away Aurelia's fear for just a moment. She shot a quizzical glance in the direction of the wall but didn't dare approach the place to verify the housekeeper's claim.

"It wasn't body parts," she finally said. "It was a single body part, a right humerus. Small, probably belonged to a woman since the muscle attachments sites aren't so prominent, but I would need to see the pelvis to be sure. An older woman — there were signs of osteoarthritis and eburnation — " She stopped abruptly, frowning.

"I wager you know what osteoarthritis is," Holmes whispered to me. "Eburnation refers to the erosion of cartilage bones, which then leads to bone-on-bone contact and gives the surface a shiny look."

"You're an insufferable know-it-all," I muttered.

If Holmes had planned a retaliatory response, he never got the chance to say it because Aurelia's momentary calm disappeared. Whatever macabre realization had halted her osteological assessment now made her wail loudly. Large, pearly tears ran down her cheeks, and the initial horror on her face turned into melancholy.

"Oh, Ruth, I'm so sorry," she lamented.

I wanted to know who Ruth was, but now was not the time for inquiry. As Aurelia's sobs became more and more deplorable, Alejo looked back at the house — perhaps paranoid that Mr. Richardson would storm the grounds suddenly and reprimand him — then heaved his charge to her feet and gently nudged her towards the door. Aurelia obliged but held onto Mrs. Hudson's hand tightly. Her crying could be heard even as the trio went back inside and down the hallway. In fact, it reached its zenith there as it had done earlier. Adding to this was Mr. Richardson's loud voice and his wife's exasperated one. I lingered in the kitchen awkwardly, listening to this medley of indiscernible sounds with Roksanda and Aurora.

"Oh, great," Aurora groaned, standing. "Dad's probably rethinking going to Milan with Aurelia in this state. But he doesn't realize she'll be better off getting a week without Portia. If he cancels, she'll throw a tantrum every day and target Aurelia for sure. I'd better go persuade him."

It was only after she had left that I noticed Holmes' absence. *Where had he disappeared off to?* I wondered. Had he left with Alejo and Mrs. Hudson to lend a hand? Or had he slipped away for some other purpose? I looked back at the yard, feeling slighted, but there was no sign of him there. It was unfortunate that Sherlock Holmes was solitary by nature; including me in his plans seemed to require extra effort on his part, and he dared not expend his energy unnecessarily like that.

The housekeeper either hadn't noticed Holmes' disappearance or wasn't curious enough to care. Her nose crinkled; the scent of Aurora's perfume, which still permeated the air, obviously repulsed her.

"She just wants a week without her stepmother in her face," she muttered.

"Are you saying that Aurora doesn't really care about her sister?" I asked.

Roksanda shot a glance at the door. Satisfied that the voices from the hallway had faded, she replied in confident tones, "I'm not saying she doesn't. I'm just saying Aurora cares more about herself than other people."

"Mrs. Hudson seems to genuinely like her."

"Well, of course, she does. She practically raised her, so she doesn't see her faults. Even if she does, she ignores them and thinks Aurora is the sweetest girl in the world."

"Why is she here anyway? Where's her husband?"

Roksanda shrugged. "The family's been pretty hush-hush about that. Aurora just showed up one day, last February I think, all distraught. From what I've overheard, her husband, David, doesn't want to have kids, but Aurora does. When she got pregnant, David gave her an ultimatum: their marriage or the baby. She chose the latter and moved back home."

"Wow, this David sounds like a real—" I started.

"Please don't give Aurora too much credit. She's rotten to the core, but I only work here so it's none of my business."

Roksanda's animosity towards her employer's daughter had been apparent from the start, so I wasn't surprised to see the bitter look that coloured her face. Whatever the root cause was, I was sure her twang of jealousy, which was obvious from the way she had eyed Aurora's purchases, only made matters worse. Even though I suspected this had nothing to do with the strange happenings that had brought us to the Richardsons' home, I had been on the verge of inquiring when I felt a tap on my shoulder. Holmes had surreptitiously materialized in the kitchen.

"Where did you—" Roksanda began.

"I had to use the loo," he replied, but I knew he was lying. He tried to appear nonchalant, yet I sensed a suppressed excitement. The subtle way his deep-set eyes danced, the hint of perspiration on his broad forehead, the slight twitch that ran through his fingers—here, my examination came to a stop. I managed to get a good look at his fingers before my scrutiny was noticed and I was forced to avert my gaze. There were smudges of dirt on the tips of some of them, but I hadn't seen him touch anything in the yard.

"If you have some time to spare, I would like to ask you a couple of questions," Holmes said to Roksanda, who consulted her watch.

"Well, I have to get started on lunch, but I guess I can talk for ten minutes."

We seated ourselves at the table once again. Holmes was now visibly excited. Roksanda, on the other hand, looked tired although the clock hadn't even struck noon yet.

Holmes began, "How long have you worked here?"

"A little over a year and a half. After graduation, I went from one intern position to the next and didn't land myself a single full-time job in my field, so when Martha told me the

Richardsons were looking—wait, why are you asking me this? What does it have to do with anything?"

Holmes frowned. "I am simply trying to see if you can give me the reliable data I need. The longer you have worked here, the more you know about this household and its occupants. Things have changed since Mrs. H's time here, so the accuracy of her information is questionable. I trust the rest of this conversation will have no more of these unproductive interruptions?"

"Uh—"

"Good. Next question then. Earlier, Mrs. H mentioned Aurelia was brought to the house in January. How would you describe her during the first month of her stay?"

"Quiet. Well, vacant really. She usually sat in the library, reading, but sometimes doing nothing in particular. Mr. Richardson often sat with her. Once she became more comfortable, she started to wander around the house. She took her medication without a fight, ate her meals, went for walks in the snow with Alejo. She didn't give anyone any trouble, although that didn't stop Mrs. Richardson from bullying—"

"The first of her episodes began in September, according to Mrs. H. Is that correct?" After a confirmatory nod from the housekeeper, Holmes went on, "Please describe this incident and provide as many details as you can."

Roksanda took a moment to recollect her thoughts. "It happened late one night. I had taken over looking after Aurelia that day because Alejo had asked for the day off. I put her to bed and went to sleep in the adjoining room where Alejo normally sleeps. The next morning, she was gone. We found her in the yard, furiously digging. It was the first of her excavations, and Mr. Richardson decided to humour her. I knew she was an archaeologist, but she'd never done anything like that—"

"For the record, Dr. Richardson was an anthropologist, not an archaeologist. Her speciality was human evolution," Holmes interrupted. "And yes, there is a difference. I've read a number of her papers. Science and history have lost a formidable scholar." He sighed. "Did her nightly escapades become a regular occurrence?"

Roksanda shook her head. "It didn't happen often, but we didn't always find her in the yard when it did. One time, we found her in a closet, crying, and then things got worse—she started hallucinating."

"And she didn't do so before September during her time in this house?"

"Not that I'd heard of."

"Hm. Did she describe what she saw?"

Roksanda shifted uncomfortably. "Uh, too vividly for my taste."

"Do share." There was an excited hunger in Holmes' eyes. Even I leaned in, hanging on to every word.

"She saw t-terrible things—bones, bodies, dead people," the housekeeper said with a shudder. "Exactly like what happened in the yard just now. I guess I would be reduced to tears too if I saw all that."

"And did she mention this Ruth character before?"

"She did, many times, but—er—I don't know who she is."

Holmes looked pensive. "So years of progress and healing are abruptly cut short. The question is what happened in September."

Roksanda shrugged. "Nothing happened."

"Not one thing out of the ordinary happened?"

"I'm telling you, nothing happened. Life was as it always was. Mrs. Richardson was planning her next vacation, Aurora went on shopping sprees, Mr. Richardson thought only about work and Aurelia, and I cooked and cleaned."

"Hm, that is most suggestive."

"Suggestive of what?" I asked.

"Isn't it obvious?" Holmes exclaimed. "The event that triggered Aurelia's relapse happened sometime before September. It led to subtle behavioural changes at first, which went unnoticed, and eventually, its impact manifested itself more noticeably." He turned to the housekeeper. "Did anything of interest happen over the spring or summer?"

Roksanda shrugged, much to Holmes' annoyance. He impatiently drummed his fingers on the table, perhaps in an attempt to intimidate the woman into talking, but it seemed she had no clue to offer.

"Aurora moved back in in February," I piped in.

"Ah! Did a disagreement about the pregnancy result in her leaving her husband?" Holmes asked prophetically. Seeing our amazement, he explained, "It is obvious. I estimate Aurora is near the end of her third trimester, which would put conception in February. She happens to move back home in February. Thus, it is not unreasonable to assume that the pregnancy was the source of some disagreement between husband and wife."

It made perfect sense now that he had explained his train of thought, for me at least. Roksanda, on the other hand, nodded but wore an expression so strange that I had no idea how to interpret it.

"Did Aurora's presence affect Aurelia in any way?" I asked her.

"Um, I don't think so," Roksanda replied. "They didn't interact much. Like Mrs. Richardson, Aurora prefers to shop and dine her way through life, so the two sisters didn't run into each other often. Even when they did, I don't remember that causing any changes in Aurelia's behaviour."

"Were there any visitors?" I asked, but there had been none. "Was Aurelia taken anywhere aside from her usual walks around the neighbourhood?" Again, Roksanda shook her head.

Holmes suddenly leaned across the table and picked up Aurelia's untouched cup of cocoa. He sniffed it, tilted the contents into his mouth, savoured the flavour for a moment, and then gulped down the rest of the drink.

Roksanda gaped at him, and I shifted awkwardly in my seat and muttered, "I thought we're supposed to be investigating."

"I am always investigating, Watson," Holmes replied. His lips smacked against each other in gustatory satisfaction, and his tongue made an odd sound as he tasted the remnants of cocoa in his mouth. Then, he said, "Something out of the ordinary did happen over the summer—the renovation. I don't understand how such a thing slipped your mind, Roksanda, since your domain, the kitchen, was greatly impacted by this. Tell me all about it and spare no details."

The housekeeper was naturally too surprised to obey this command right away. "How did you know that? Did Martha tell you?"

Holmes waved away her question impatiently and motioned for her to answer his. Yet, it was apparent that she would not be menaced into responding. I liked her for it.

94

However, Holmes possessed the uncanny ability to command people (the Baker House bullies were an unfortunate exception), and defiance usually meant consequences for the disobeyer — that is, he or she would be subjected to watch Holmes transform into a grimacing, angry child. At that moment, for example, his thin lips pouted in displeasure, his eyes became slits, and he refused to utter a single word. Hence, I interjected, albeit diffidently.

"Um, compared to the other parts of the house we've seen so far, everything in the kitchen looks new, including the paint job, so this room's been remodeled recently."

Holmes nodded in approval, although it was needless to say that he had noticed details that no amount of scrutiny on my part could ever pick up. I looked at him helplessly, having nothing more to add. He offered no elaboration, however. Luckily, the housekeeper's bewildered expression had relaxed, and she spoke before Holmes could start grumbling.

"Yeah, the kitchen was renovated, along with other parts of the house. It happened back in June and lasted for about three weeks. I didn't think to mention it because Aurelia was fine despite all the extra noise and contractors in and out of the house. She kept to herself most of the time, either in her room or in the library."

"Exactly which parts of the house were renovated?" Holmes asked.

"Apart from the kitchen, Mr. and Mrs. Richardson's bedroom and one of the guest bedrooms. The basement and the attic were also cleaned out and given a paint job. They also did some interior waterproofing for the basement because we've been having flooding problems during heavy rains."

Holmes' eyes lit up. "Ah, that explains the curious detail I noted earlier. Tell me about the painting."

"The painting?" Roksanda asked, raising an eyebrow.

"The one that was discovered in the basement and currently hangs in the hallway that leads to this room."

The housekeeper's mouth hung open. "How did you—?"

"It is my business to know things. These interruptions really are becoming a nuisance. Please just answer the question."

Roksanda looked at me, as though expecting me to succeed where she had failed, but I kept silent. Holmes, I could see, was both aroused and agitated, and although he usually relished the prospect of astounding his audience with his astute deductions, sometimes he was more interested in the solution rather than the performance. Right now, he was eager for answers, so I gave Roksanda a nod, encouraging her to oblige—before his irritation made him diagnose her of another disease.

"We were cleaning out the basement so that the contractors could begin the waterproofing," Roksanda began, after a sigh. "Everyone was there, except Aurora. Aurelia watched; Mr. Richardson, Alejo, and I did the bulk of the work, and Mrs. Richardson supervised, although she spent most of the time complaining about how frugal Mr. Richardson is.

"I was the one who discovered the painting — a barren forest landscape, carelessly wrapped and stored away in one of the closets. I thought it was a bit depressing to look at, and there was some water damage, so I was about to put it in the discard pile when Mrs. Richardson saw it. She loved it and insisted that it be put on display, and that's why it's hanging on the wall right now."

"How did Aurelia react to the painting when she first saw it?" Holmes asked.

"I could tell she didn't like it very much. It's a bit on the gloomy side, as I said. At first, she would only avert her gaze when she had to walk down the hallway. I think she just pretended it wasn't there, and then almost overnight, she became a mess every time she had to enter the hallway."

"Almost overnight, eh. Intriguing! So why wasn't it taken down?"

"Because Mrs. Richardson will throw a tantrum if that happens and her tantrums are worse than Aurelia's episodes. I think she secretly enjoys seeing Aurelia like this. She's probably hoping Mr. Richardson will have her institutionalized again."

"How horrible," I murmured.

Holmes nodded his agreement, although his face retained its usual cool detachment from anything that even vaguely resembled an emotion.

"Poor Mr. Richardson," Roksanda went on, shaking her head. "He's trying to save his daughter and please his wife, and he thinks he can do both. Ever since the painting started upsetting Aurelia, she's been getting her meals served in her room or the library, so that she doesn't need to pass it to get to the kitchen or dining room. If she wants to go into the yard, Alejo takes her through the front door and around the property. I think today, with all that business with the rope, he forgot and tried to take Aurelia down the hall. You both saw how that ended."

After an uncomfortable pause, which I involuntarily spent reliving Aurelia's terrified shrieks, Roksanda looked at Holmes and said timidly, "Are you going to tell us how you knew about the pain—"

"No," came the abrupt answer.

The housekeeper stood up, wearing an expression that was almost as stern as Mrs. Hudson's. "In that case, I need to start making lunch, and you need to leave my kitchen."

"There is nothing left to do here anyway. Let us return to Baker House, Watson," Holmes said, and not wasting another moment, without pause for a "goodbye" or a "thank you", he marched out of the kitchen. Offering an apologetic half-smile to Roksanda, I scurried after him.

Chapter 7 The Evidence

"A cast of your skull, sir, until the original is available, would be an ornament to any anthropological museum."

—Sir Arthur Conan Doyle, *The Hound of the Baskervilles*

DURING THE BUS RIDE TO BAKER HOUSE, HOLMES sank into his seat in a contemplative mood and said very little, which was unfortunate since I was eager to discuss the day's events. With considerable effort, I managed to provoke a brief conversation.

"Isn't it strange that the housekeeper is more worried about Aurelia than her own father?" I asked.

Holmes raised a brow. "You think Alistair Richardson doesn't care about his daughter?"

"He refuses to have her institutionalized."

"There can be a number of innocent reasons for that, Watson. However, the point you raise is peculiar."

"I'd say the stepmother is also suspicious," I went on. "I wouldn't be surprised if she was sabotaging Aurelia's recovery."

"Sabotaging, eh?" Holmes said. "How do you propose she is doing that?"

"Scare tactics, of course. The painting in the hallway, for example. She purposely chose to hang it there even though it upsets Aurelia. If she loves the painting so much, why not hang it in her own bedroom? She choose that spot because Aurelia needs to pass it to get to the kitchen and dining room. I don't think she cares about that painting at all."

"Excellent theory, Watson. You may be onto something."

"Really?"

"Oh, yes. Now be quiet, will you? I need to think."

I ignored this and continued with my suspect list. "Now that nurse—he's also somewhat suspicious."

Holmes looked irritated but didn't object when I carried on.

"He told Mr. Richardson that he was taking a smoke break when Aurelia tried to hang herself, but did you notice that he came from the second floor when he rescued her? If he'd stepped outside for a smoke, he would've needed to pass us to get to the second floor."

"Indeed," Holmes said thoughtfully. "So you have an eye for detail after all. Have the sister and the housekeeper made it onto your suspect list as well? Do you suspect Mrs. H too?" He chuckled softly. "You can tell me your theories later, if you don't mind."

I did mind, very much in fact. But he resumed his reticence anyway, and no amount of persuasion on my part could prompt further discussion. Hence, I made it my mission to extract his thoughts at a later time. I would, of course, have to introduce the topic with subtlety and disinterest since Holmes was the most stubborn person I knew. If he had set his mind on burying himself inside the pages of his chemistry textbook all afternoon, neither pleading nor threats would persuade him to do otherwise.

Once we arrived at Baker House, we parted ways, agreeing to meet in his room in two hours' time. The enchantment of the Richardsons' home had worn off somewhat by the time I unlocked my second-floor bedroom, unit 2C. The memories of Aurelia's shrieks, the scent of Alejo's cigarettes, and Mr. Richardson's stern face became distant, and I felt an odd sense of relief at the sight of my humble abode. My room was nothing more than a large closet fitted with a four-pane sliding sash window, a neat bed and desk, and a small, wooden chest of drawers. Yet there was a calm here that was absent from the extraordinary home I had spent the morning in.

After taking a long shower, I made a salad in the kitchen and loitered by the bay windows of the living room, watching passersby and engaging in small talk with a fellow student, before heading to Holmes' room at the appointed time. With my copy of *The Victorian Frame of Mind*, a notebook, and a pen at hand, my disguise of eager-to-study Watson was complete.

Holmes' sanctum sanctorum—unit 2B—sat next door to mine. Although slightly larger than mine, one often developed claustrophobia upon entering since his was a room chockablock with paraphernalia. In addition to the furniture provided by the university, Holmes had installed an armchair, a floor lamp, and a very large bookcase that took up more than half the length of one wall. All five shelves were stacked with books, old newspapers, and odd playthings only he knew the purpose of. The curtains were usually undone, and the floor lamp was often on the lowest setting, which cast the room in grey shadows. The only form of decor Holmes permitted was a poster of the periodic table—if that can be considered decor—which he had pasted on the wall across from his bed. I didn't know why he bothered since he could already recite the elements in the order of their atomic number (he had done this one rainy evening when I had complained of boredom—I had been far from amused). I supposed he liked waking up to see the poster.

A muffled "come in" beckoned me when I knocked. I entered to find Holmes sitting at his desk, which looked remarkably clean save for a rack of half-filled test tubes and a lit Bunsen burner that had been placed under a tripod. A beaker filled halfway with simmering liquid sat on top.

"Uh, I'm pretty sure you're not allowed to have that stuff in the house," I said.

Holmes smiled mischievously. "I trust you won't tell. Experimentation is a far more efficient way of learning than reading a textbook, although I am fond of doing that too."

"I'm sure it is. Just make sure you don't set your room on fire. Where did you get all that stuff anyway?"

"I borrowed them from the lab," he said simply and returned to studying the beaker.

"You mean you stole them?"

"It is not theft if one has every intention of returning the items. Make yourself comfortable on the bed."

This was not an easy thing to do since Holmes had transferred the contents of his desk to the bed, which was already cluttered with a thick, rumpled comforter. Half of it lay on the floor and the other half was buried under books, a stack of newspapers, an empty pop can, and a highlighter with a missing lid. I surveyed the armchair by the window, but it housed a stack of heavy books. Sighing, I pushed some of the books on the bed aside and settled in as comfortably as I could but only after opening the curtains and flooding the room with sunlight — a gesture which annoyed Holmes, although he didn't complain out loud. We worked (and I ate) without quarreling for nearly twenty minutes. That was when Holmes did something that made me put my book down.

Reaching into his backpack, which lay by his feet, he pulled out a human skull that had been neatly wrapped in a clear plastic bag. Over the past few weeks, I had seen all sorts of strange props emerge from that backpack, but this had been the oddest (and creepiest) thing by far. Despite the fact that it was a plastic imitation, I didn't like the way the hollow eye sockets bore into mine.

"It is real, you know," Holmes said, grinning as broadly as the skull.

I straightened jerkily and my book fell to my lap, forgotten. "What! That can't be — it's real?"

"Oh, yes. Male, late teens, of Indian ancestry, purchased by the university in the 1970s."

"You stole a skull from the anthropology lab!"

"Borrowed," Holmes corrected. "I am considering doing a minor in anthropology, Watson. Fascinating subject! The biological subfield anyway. This specimen is integral to my paper on age estimation and cranial suture closure." He gently pulled the skull out of the bag and rested it on his palm. "As you can see, despite being an adolescent, the sutures — "

Here, he pointed to the faded squiggly lines that ran up and down and side to side on the cranium, " — are in an advanced stage of fusion. The forensic application — "

I had little interest in sutures, however. "How did you know about the painting?" I blurted out.

This was not how I had intended to introduce the topic, but had I let Holmes continue, he would have given an hour-long sermon on bones, which I was in no mood to hear. Unfortunately, instead of answering, he put down the skull with deliberate slowness on the desk, pulled out a magnifying glass from one of the drawers, and began scrutinizing the sutures he had pointed out.

Five minutes passed before I sighed in surrender. "If I remember correctly from one of your previous rants — I mean, *discussions* — on forensic anthropology, sutures generally close with age, which is why anthropologists use them to estimate the age of a skull, but it's not a very reliable technique."

Holmes' face remained as impassive as ever, but his lips stretched slightly — into a smile? He put down the magnifying glass and looked at me.

"Ah, so you do pay attention when I try to educate you. You usually look rather vacant, so I assumed that nothing I say penetrates your skull. You know, oral recitation is a good way of preparing for exams, which is why I do it. You can lecture me on Victorian literature, if you please."

I couldn't help but laugh as I envisioned his face if I were to soliloquize my thoughts on Dickens or Austen. "Maybe another day, Holmes. Right now, you have some explaining to do."

"I suppose I do. I wouldn't want you to implode from an unsatiated curiosity." He cleared his throat loudly. "How did I know about the painting? The answer is simple. From Aurelia's reaction to the painting in the hallway, which you correctly identified, it was apparent that it has some role to play in the story. I knew it was a relatively recent addition to the wall. If you had looked carefully at the wall, you would have seen the faint outlines of frames, indicating how the paintings had been previously arranged. A rearrangement occurred to make room for the new one.

"Second, there were signs of water damage along one side of the painting, which the Richardsons had tried to conceal by choosing a wide frame. However, the damage is apparent if you look closely, and so I deduced that the painting had been carelessly stored in a moist environment, or had suffered water damage through other means, and was put up without reparation. When Roksanda mentioned waterproofing the basement, I speculated that the painting had been uncovered there, which she confirmed."

I pondered this information for a moment and then asked, "And why did you drink Aurelia's cocoa?"

"Because I was thirsty and the housekeeper didn't offer any refreshments. Quite rude of her actually."

I glared at him suspiciously. "That's a bunch of bull—"

"Language, Watson. I admit I did have a motive apart from quenching my thirst." Holmes paused for dramatic effect, and I waited patiently for him to go on. "I was checking to see if the drink had been laced with something."

I gasped. "Why on earth would you think that—wait, does that mean you suspect Roksanda?"

"One must not point fingers before sufficient evidence is accumulated. I was simply testing a theory."

"Since you haven't fainted or acting stranger than usual, I'm assuming the cocoa was clean."

Holmes nodded.

I was quiet for a moment. I gazed at Holmes—at his old-fashioned dress, then at his young face. He was very young—*we* were very young, too young and possibly too foolish to play detective. Had we fallen prey to our overactive imaginations and the superstitions of an old lady? I remembered the way we had been scrutinized at the Richardsons' home. Suddenly, the entire investigation felt silly.

"There's an alternative to consider," I began slowly. "Maybe there's no mystery here."

I had expected a high-pitched, indignant response from Holmes, but he regarded me coolly and said softly, "You don't think we are dealing with a mystery?"

I shrugged. "What exactly are we investigating? A woman whose health is deteriorating? A father in denial? A possibly evil stepmother?"

"You forgot Mrs. H's theory of a demonic presence," Holmes said, grinning.

I snorted. "Those were not her words, but that would spice things up. I won't hold my breath though. Unless we stalk the Richardsons by hiding out in the bushes, watch the house, and catch someone doing something fishy, I won't believe there's a mystery here."

"What a capital idea! Imagine if we could fly out of that window, hover over the Richardson house, gently remove the roof, and peep inside—how revelatory that would be! If we could do that, I would certainly be able to convince you, Watson, that something foul is at work."

"Does 'foul' imply something supernatural?"

"There is nothing more unnatural than the commonplace. But let me assure you, the mystery is mostly cleared up."

I raised a brow, and Holmes smiled ominously. Contrary to the usual silence that followed any time he said something cryptic, he opened his mouth as though he were about to offer a scrap to quench my curiosity. But I always did have the worst luck in these matters. Holmes' phone, which rarely made a sound, rang that day.

"I shall be right back," he said, and promptly exited the room, leaving me alone with a grinning skull and a simmering beaker that was starting to emit a disturbing odour.

I returned to *The Victorian Frame of Mind* unhappily, my mind contemplating Holmes' mysterious caller and his abrupt exit. By the time he returned twenty minutes later, I had convinced myself that his mother had called, although her existence was questionable, and had taken a page of notes for my essay. This was no accomplishment since my writing was obnoxiously large and messy. The book was captivating though, and I had been quite immersed in it when I happened to look up to find Holmes holding two cups of espresso.

"Oh, I don't have caffeine after three," I said grudgingly, after glancing at the time on my phone. The strong scent had already drifted teasingly up my nostrils, but I resisted the temptation to snatch the drink.

"I am aware," Holmes replied. "They are both for me." He drank them in quick succession and then added in an explanatory tone, "Lunch."

As though two espressos qualified as a meal replacement! But I supposed coffee was better than an empty stomach, which was usually the case when Holmes was extremely excited about something. This was precisely the state he was in now. There was a sparkle in his eyes and a subtle urgency in the way he paced the room—I was sure the caffeine hadn't kicked in yet.

"I trust you are not busy this evening?" he asked.

"It's the weekend. Of course, I have plans," I answered as convincingly as I could.

"Ah, *c'est dommage*. We have been called to the Richardson house by Mrs. H." He didn't look disappointed at the prospect of returning to the investigation alone; had he guessed that I had nothing planned that night except for homework and perhaps a book?

"Did something happen?" I inquired.

"Thankfully, no. Mrs. H is being paranoid though. Mr. and Mrs. Richardson are leaving for Milan this evening, and when Roksanda leaves for the day, only Dr. Richardson, the sister, and the nurse will be in the house. Mrs. H's exact words were 'I feel we are sailing close to the wind, Sherlock. I would feel better if you and Ms. Watson were here.' Although I don't understand what sailing has to do with her feelings of impending danger—"

"It's an idiom, Holmes."

"Ah, I see. The artful aspects of English are your domain, mate, not mine. I have more important information to fill my brain att—"

"What else did Mrs. Hudson say?"

"She would like us to spend the night. She will be present as well. She has also arranged a rendezvous that will no doubt be informative, but I won't bore you with the details since you will be otherwise preoccupied."

"Um, well, I'm sure I can reschedule—" I began.

"How fortunate," Holmes said. I could tell by his sarcastic tone that he had seen through my ruse with very little effort. After all, he gauged the most peculiar details of strangers from a single glance. I wasn't surprised that he had read me like a book, but I blushed, nonetheless. However, despite his occasional bursts of sarcasm and callousness, there was a part of him that was sensitive and kind, for he added, "It would be good to have you by my side, Watson."

I shifted uncomfortably at the compliment. "Er, so who's the rendezvous with?"

"Dr. Aurelia Richardson," he answered.

"Aurelia? But she doesn't talk much."

"I believe I can persuade her. We have much to discuss."

"And how do you plan to do that?"

Holmes grinned, his face looking as mischievous as the skull. "You will have to wait and see, my friend." With that, he seated himself at the desk and began scrutinizing the contents of the beaker.

"Do you smell that?" he asked a moment later. "The experiment is coming along nicely. I am sure Professor Deward will be happy with this."

It didn't bother me that he was speaking to the skull rather than me. What was disturbing was the relish in his voice. I frantically prayed that he would refrain from taking a swig of the murky yellow liquid in the beaker.

*

Armed with a backpack containing my pajamas, toiletries, and a book, which I figured there would be no time to read but felt inclined to pack, I waited outside Baker House for Holmes. I had wrongly assumed that Holmes had been holed up in his room all evening, playing with his chemistry set, since there had been no response when I had knocked on his door. Perhaps an excursion—something to do with the case?—had pulled him away from his favourite four walls. Surprisingly, this notion irritated me. With nothing to distract me but a small street lined with a long row of Victorian homes and mid-rise apartments—all cast in shadows since the sun had set nearly four hours before—I fidgeted and paced, eyeing a vague semblance of students who stood chatting in front of a fraternity house some distance away.

A few minutes later as the clock struck nine, Holmes ambled leisurely out of Baker House to find a snappy, shivery me, rigorously marching to and fro.

"Where were you?" I demanded. "I knocked on your door."

Holmes shrugged nonchalantly. "Oh, did you? I was occupied with a riveting article on —"

"Not interested," I growled.

The walk to the Richardson's home was a silent one. The only time there was chitchat was when I suggested taking the bus as the cold worsened and Holmes rebuked it. He picked up his pace, and I followed suit grudgingly. When we arrived, there was sweat trickling down my back since I had worn both a jacket and a thick sweater. Holmes, on the other hand, looked pristine, which made me wonder if he had discovered some mechanism for moderating his body temperature — without odiously sweating like the rest of humanity, of course.

Mrs. Hudson let us into the house. The place was eerily quiet. We were informed that Mr. and Mrs. Richardson had left to catch their flight, and Roksanda had gone home for the day, her shift having ended four hours earlier. Although I wasn't expecting it, Aurora didn't come out to greet us. In fact, I was quite sure this invitation to spend the night in her father's home would have infuriated her. Somehow, the old housekeeper, either through charm or maternal strictness, had prevailed, and here we were.

We were led into the exquisite foyer, the sight of which instantly warmed me up, and down the left-hand hallway. *Where are we going?* I wondered. A quick glance at Holmes told me he knew exactly where we were headed, but I too found out when Mrs. Hudson came to an abrupt stop. Before us stood a pair of impressive oak doors. Decorated with simple floral engravings and golden doorknobs, it was the very picture of antiquity. I quivered with excitement.

"The library," I croaked once we were ushered inside.

"Try not to drool," Holmes murmured, laughing.

I was too baffled by the interior of the room to come up with a rude response. The library was styled to match the rest of the house — dark wood panelling for the walls and rows and rows of cherry oak shelves filled with books. A few portraits decorated the walls, and a glittering chandelier hung from the ceiling. Off to one corner was an unlit fireplace — a real one rather than those abysmal electric ones — and a wooden coffee table, around which couches had been arranged in a semi-circle. I barely heard Mrs. Hudson shut the door behind us; I could have stood there admiring the site for the next hour. Holmes, perhaps realizing this, took my arm and steered me towards the couches.

"Where's Mrs. Hud—"

"She has gone to fetch Dr. Rich— oh, please don't sit there, Watson," Holmes said just as I was about to make myself comfortable on the armchair. "I wouldn't want you to damage the evidence."

I froze, and then straightening, looked quizzically at the armchair. It appeared to be an ordinary couch — modern and expensive, a deep sapphire blue velvety exterior sitting on a solid wood base. How on earth was this evidence? I voiced the question out loud.

"Not the sofa. What a ridiculous assumption! I was referring to what lies beneath the seat cushion. Step aside, Watson."

He nudged me aside gently, and standing in my place, removed the seat cushion. Very carefully, he picked up something and whirled around to show me. My eyes must have bulged in alarm; my mouth definitely hung open for a moment before I forced it shut. How else could I have reacted to the unsavory sight of a dirty, yellow bone?

Chapter 8 The Rendezvous

I do not think that I have ever seen such deadly paleness in a woman's face.

—Sir Arthur Conan Doyle, *The Adventure of the Beryl Coronet*

ONE HUNDRED THOUGHTS, MOSTLY IN THE FORM of questions, bombarded my head. Had Holmes "borrowed" another specimen from the anthropology lab? But the terrible state of the bone contradicted this; I was sure the folks at the anthropology department kept their specimens in immaculate condition. I supposed Holmes could have caused the bone's pitiful state, although this was difficult to imagine. Sherlock Holmes may have been impatient and unkind to the living, but he treated the dead with the utmost respect. I had seen the way he handled bones in the lab, as though they were treasures of the greatest value. Even if he had done nothing to the bone, why had he brought it into the Richardsons' home and how had it ended up in the library—a room neither of us had visited before? And then, I remembered something.

"Did you explore the house under the pretense of using the bathroom earlier?" I asked.

Holmes smiled. "Guilty. Judging by your expression, which is mingled with confusion and disgust, I believe that you think this bone is real."

"It looks real," I argued.

"And how would an English major who has never even held a real bone know that?" Without waiting for my rebuttal, he continued matter-of-factly, "It is a cheap plastic imitation. What is curious is how it fooled Dr. Richardson with all her years of osteological expertise. She clearly didn't touch it. The surface texture and weight would have easily exposed it as a fake. Still, she should have seen that the olecranon fossa is missing." Turning the bone, he remarked, "And no nutrient foramen or greater tub—"

"She's sick, Holmes. Do you expect her to remember all this jargon?"

"I suppose you are right."

Although a few seconds late, my brain finally registered what Holmes had said. "Wait a minute! Are you saying that Aurelia did dig up a bone in the backyard today and this was that bone?"

Holmes' answer was a vague movement of the head. In fact, it was imperceptible enough that I couldn't tell if it was a nod or a shake. The gesture irritated me beyond measure.

"Give me an answer right now or I'm going home." My language had been a bit more colourful than the words expressed on this page. In my defence, profanity was sometimes the push Holmes needed to compel him to talk. Startled by my threat, he cleared his throat and tried to look as placating as possible.

"The answer to both of your questions is yes. She was not hallucinating as the others had thought," he said.

I remembered all the household objects that had lain partly exposed in the yard. "So she buried a bone, then uncovered it, and got scared to death by it? That makes no — wait! Maybe the bone was planted in the yard to scare Aurelia?"

"My thoughts exactly."

"Who would do such a thing?"

"I am more concerned with the 'why' rather than the 'who'."

I thought the "who" was quite important. In this case, it was also deeply disturbing since only someone who was aware of Aurelia's digs would know when and where to plant the bone. Without a doubt, whoever had done it was a member of the Richardson household. But further discussion on this point was fruitless since Holmes seemed unconcerned about this.

I asked instead, "How did you find it when Roksanda couldn't?"

Holmes chuckled and stroked the bone affectionately. "Telling you would spoil the fun. Be patient, Watson."

There was no time to threaten him with leaving again because the doors sprung open, and Mrs. Hudson and a timid-looking Aurelia entered. When I turned back to look at Holmes, I saw that he had gracefully seated himself in the armchair, the bone nowhere to be seen.

Mrs. Hudson settled Aurelia on the matching loveseat, squeezed her shoulder reassuringly, and left without saying a word. I took my seat somewhat nervously next to Aurelia, and the interrogation began.

"Good evening, Dr. Richardson," Holmes said warmly. We didn't receive any salutations in return. Aurelia hadn't lifted her gaze from the floor since entering the room, but there was a nearly imperceptible nod of the head and a fleeting smile. Holmes went on, "We met earlier today as you no doubt recall, but we were not properly introduced."

This, I realized, was true; we hadn't taken the time to exchange pleasantries with her even during the relatively calm period spent in her presence in the kitchen. Even though we wouldn't have received any acknowledgement had we done so, I still felt ashamed.

"I am Sherlock Holmes and this is my friend, Janah Watson. We are students at the university.

Mrs. H—er—Martha told me that you completed your graduate studies there in anthropology."

Aurelia fidgeted in her seat but remained silent.

"Watson and I are here in an investigatory capacity at the request of Mrs. H, who is extremely worried about you." He paused, studying the woman. "Your health is declining, rather suddenly. Do you know what is sabotaging your recovery?"

All of her subtle, involuntary movements stopped; even her breathing seemed to slow down. I sensed fear in her rigidity. Was she being unresponsive as usual, or had she clearly understood Holmes' question but was too frightened to speak?

"What are you afraid of, Aurelia?" I asked softly.

I was acknowledged with a fleeting glance and a mumbled response, "Them."

Holmes sat back and motioned for me to continue. For some odd reason, Aurelia had chosen to respond to me.

"Who is 'them'? Are you referring to your family or someone else?" I asked apprehensively. I tried to sound as gentle as possible, but the anxious, raised pitch of my voice was noticeable.

"They're haunting me," came the woman's cryptic response.

I decided to play along. "Were they haunting you when you lived at the hospital?"

"In the beginning, yes."

"And were they haunting you when you moved here in January?"

Aurelia was still for a moment. I was starting to think I had lost my new-found ability to make her talk when she shook her head.

"When did they start haunting you again?"

No response. Instead, I saw the poor woman quiver, eyes brightening with tears unshed. I decided to switch to another topic, but it wasn't any less sensitive.

"Is someone in this house trying to hurt you?" I asked.

Aurelia nodded slowly. "There are f-four of them. Bu–but it's okay. I accept it. I deserve it."

My mouth, which had been open, ready to hammer out my next question, remained that way as I digested Aurelia's response. Four people? I shot Holmes a look, but his returning glance was as bewildered as mine.

"Can you tell me who these four people are?"

"You look so much like her," Aurelia murmured. She had a knack for not answering the questions I wanted the answers to most, but her reply made me blink in surprise, nonetheless.

"Like who?"

"Kalinda. You look so much like Kalinda." A single tear rolled down Aurelia's face. I wondered if my resemblance to this Kalinda person was the reason my questions had been answered whereas Holmes' had been ignored.

As a second tear trickled down her cheek, I asked, "Where did you find the rope that you — uh — the rope that you tied to the handrail today — where did you get it?"

"It was already tied to the handrail."

I stiffened hearing this. Planting a bone in the yard had been a cold-hearted thing to do, but the rope implied serious harm, even death. Had the same person been responsible for both deeds? "Do you know who put it there?"

"They did."

"And why would *they* do that?"

Aurelia looked tearful again, but there was another emotion on her face. Was it shame? "Because that's how the Place predicted I would die."

I was speechless. Even Holmes gaped at the woman with surprise and fresh curiosity. He leaned forward pressingly, lips parted, and drummed his fingers on the armrest. While he seemed to be teeming with new questions, I had no idea what to say next. We were clearly speaking to a person whose sense of reality was in ruins, perhaps even beyond repair. My appetite for humouring Aurelia gone, I shrugged helplessly at Holmes, who gave me an obliging nod. His fingers stopped their dance on the velvet, and his hands clasped one another as he sank back into the couch, eyes bright.

"Where is this Place you speak of?" he asked delicately.

No response.

"Is it on the island where your expedition took place six years ago?"

Aurelia nodded slowly.

"But you have seen the Place in more recent times, haven't you?" The question surprised me. It even made Aurelia look up, meeting Holmes' eyes for the first time since entering the library.

"Yes," she replied.

Although I was puzzled by this, Holmes seemed satisfied with her answer. "Tell me about the expedition."

One minute passed in silence, then another. Despite our patient wait, the answer we hoped for continued to evade us. Aurelia remained still, I fidgeted awkwardly, and Holmes' face, which had looked meditative at first, gradually twitched with restlessness. Perhaps that was why he reached into the side of the seat cushion and pulled out the bone he had shown me earlier. Fearing the repercussions of such an insensitive act, I glanced at Aurelia, bracing myself for a scream, a violent shout, or some other sign of a woman on the verge of madness.

Holmes' callous display had its intended effect. The poor woman looked mortified, and tears streamed down her cheeks. I stared at my feet, feeling more and more uncomfortable, as her weeping grew louder. Holmes, impassive as ever, studied her with the same scholarly interest he had shown the skull that was sitting on his desk at Baker House. I was sure he would eventually grow impatient and demand that Aurelia wipe her eyes and give straightforward answers. Luckily, Aurelia stifled her anguish and vocalized what must have been echoing inside her head, although it was neither illuminating nor unambiguous.

"I'm so sorry, Ruth," she whispered.

This was Holmes' queue to restart his interrogation, which fortunately paused the sobbing. He asked the same question I had been thinking of: "Who is Ruth?"

The answer came instantly. "My colleague."

"Is she dead?"

A loud whimper and then, "Yes."

"Did it happen during the dig?"

A nod.

"How did she die?"

Aurelia didn't answer, but the tears flowed faster than before. I silently cursed Holmes' relentless questioning as the sobbing grew loud again, and watched the door, expecting Mrs. Hudson, Aurora and Alejo to march in furiously at any moment. I pictured the muscled arms of the nurse ejecting us from the house and our shivering, pathetic figures walking moodily back to Baker House. Nothing of that sort happened, however, which unfortunate since eviction would have paled in comparison to what happened later that night.

Holmes' voice interrupted my terrible reverie. "Dr. Richardson, you must stop crying. This humerus does *not* belong to Ruth."

"Yes, it does. Older female, osteoporotic—" Aurelia began.

"This bone is fake, made of plastic."

But it seemed the distraught woman heard nothing but her own osteological recitation.

"—signs of arthritis, and the cuts—there are cuts all over that bone. Who else could it be? It's Ruth!"

Intrigued, I peered at the bone, admonishing myself for not noticing something as obvious as cut marks. However, even without a studious examination, I could see that although the bone was very dirty, the exposed yellow surface was smooth.

"Is that how Ruth died? Was she stabbed?" Holmes asked. "Multiple times, I assume, by your pluralizing of cuts."

Receiving only sobs for an answer—what else were we to expect with so gruesome a question?—Holmes waved the bone impatiently and snapped, "This is *not* real. You need to understand that. Here, hold it and you will see." He leaned over and thrust the humerus into Aurelia's hand, forcefully closing her fingers around it.

For one long minute, Aurelia sat frozen, fingers clasped tightly around the thing that had sent her into a panicked frenzy twice in one day. Her face now devoid of fear, she studied the bone in disbelief before setting it down on the coffee table. When she straightened and stood up, she looked different—her face was brighter, her body didn't fidget, and there was clarity in her eyes.

"I'm going to bed now," she said calmly and began walking towards the door.

"I would appreciate an answer to my question," Holmes called out; Aurelia stopped but didn't turn around. "How did Ruth die?"

There was a pause, followed by this terrible response: "I killed her. I killed all of them."

We remained sitting, unable to move or speak. Aurelia took the silence as her sign to leave and promptly exited the room. It was only when the door slammed shut that I took a breath.

*

"Holmes, are you still awake?" I whispered, some hours later.

"Yes," came the answer instantly, "but I am surprised that you are. A full belly and a comfortable bed are usually more than enough to make you doze off. You are worse than an infant sometimes."

"Ha, ha, very funny."

He was right on all accounts, and under normal circumstances, I would have fallen asleep minutes after snuggling into bed, especially the one I was presently in. It was nearly twice the size of mine at Baker House, covered with memory foam pillows and the softest of bedsheets. While I was nestled beneath a thick comforter, poor Holmes had graciously accepted the reclining leather chair, a single pillow, and a cotton sheet. Perhaps I had imagined it, but to my irritation, Mrs. Hudson had looked disappointed when she had found out that we would not be sharing the bed. Considering the size of the Richardson home, I was certain the old housekeeper had lied about this being the only furnished room available. Or perhaps she had been too lazy to prepare another room. It would have fallen on her to do so since Roksanda wasn't at our disposal and no one was sure where Aurora was (although it was difficult for me to picture her carrying out domestic tasks). But housekeepers are seldom lazy people in my limited experience, so I figured Mrs. Hudson was simply being a nefarious matchmaker.

I felt guilty that Holmes would be stuck in a chair all night, even though I had entered his room at Baker House more than once to find him fast asleep in his armchair. When he moved his chair to face the window and demanded the curtains remain open, I was puzzled but didn't argue. Only after settling into bed did I realize to my great annoyance that the moon, being exceptionally bright that night, streamed into the room and added a glow to everything it touched.

"You haven't said a word all evening," I complained, whispering again.

This was only a slight exaggeration. After Aurelia's departure, Holmes had remained sitting for some time, looking pensive. I didn't dare disturb him while he was thinking since an intrusion would have only elicited a rude outburst from him, and that would have provoked an even ruder rebuttal from me. Not trusting myself to remain quiet though, I had wandered over to the shelves and perused some titles in the hopes of drawing out my normally bookish self. My mind, unfortunately, had been too busy contemplating the events of the day, particularly our interview with Aurelia Richardson. All I could do was wonder how much truth her words held, and hope and pray that all of it was illusory, something imagined by a broken mind. Another part of me had entertained darker possibilities.

By the time I returned to the couch with the book I had absentmindedly plucked from a shelf, Holmes had sunk further into his seat, face fully obscured by a large, black textbook titled *Quantitative Chemical Analysis.* I wouldn't have been surprised if he had filled his "rucksack" with books instead of pajamas and a toothbrush. When he pulled out a notebook and pencil a few minutes later and began scribbling down odd notations, symbols, and numbers, I knew I had lost him to chemistry problems. By the looks of that book, there were thousands for him to solve, and he would no doubt do the assigned homework and then some more for fun.

We had remained in the library for over an hour when Mrs. Hudson brought us warmed milk (we were clearly still children in her eyes). Under her surveillant gaze, we emptied our cups before being ushered off to a room on the first floor (she now viewed us as adults old enough to share a bedroom). Although annoyed by her insinuation, I was relieved to find out that we hadn't been put in the guest bedroom upstairs next to Aurelia's room. Mrs. Hudson had taken that one. Aurelia's confession still lurked on my mind; sleeping soundly in close proximity to her would have been nearly impossible for me. Instead, we had the pleasure of sharing the floor with the less villainous sister, although Aurora hadn't been seen all evening.

Bottled-up curiosity is not good for the soul; that much was obvious from my constant fidgeting once in bed. After some time, I sat up and leaned into the pillows I had propped against the headboard. Much to my irritation, Holmes was lying very still, his moon-lit figure the picture of tranquility despite his spartan bunk. This, along with a mind that was teeming with conspiracy, was what prompted me to interrupt whatever peaceful dreams he had been in the middle of. But it seemed sleep was a rare luxury in these parts—white teeth had grinned in greeting almost immediately.

"Do you think Aurelia was telling the truth when she said she killed people?" I whispered.

"There is no need to whisper," Holmes replied. "The three occupants of the first floor — er, second floor, as you would say it here — can't hear us, and I hear nothing from Aurora's room. Either she is not home yet or she is sleeping soundly. It is past midnight after all."

I cleared my throat impatiently.

"Oh, alright. The facts suggest that Dr. Richardson killed no one."

"Have you been gathering facts without telling me again?" I asked.

I had wasted the sarcasm, however, since Holmes replied, "Obviously. I asked Mrs. H while you were busy in the bathroom." His glowing, pale face wordlessly remarked: *This is what you miss when you choose toiletries over the investigation.* He continued aloud, "To her knowledge, Dr. Richardson has not killed anyone."

"And you believe her?"

"Mrs. H has no reason to lie to us."

"So why does your face look like that?"

"Surely you can't see my face that clearly, although the moon is rather luminous tonight."

"Fine," I grumbled. "Your voice — I can hear it in your voice. You don't believe her."

Holmes responded with a quiet but blithesome laugh. "Well, Watson, I am quite flattered that you are cognizant of all the nuances of my voi — oh, but I digress." He grew grave once again. "Mrs. H only knows what she knows. Truth be told, I am not sure what to think. I would like to believe that Dr. Richardson hurt no one, but the humerus — the supposed cut marks on the humerus — now *that* is most suggestive."

Utterly perplexed, I waited for him to go on. He stared back at me incredulously. "Why, Watson, isn't it obvious? Think! Why would there be cut marks on a humerus? Why would someone get stabbed repeatedly in the arm? It makes no sense unless — unless — I can think of only one scenario, and it is gruesome." He paused for breath but that didn't ease his fitful fingers, which had started drumming on the armrest. "Imagine a feverish mind — a mind that has lost touch with reality — can you not envision that person hurting another in a mad frenzy — stabbing them without pause, blow after blow penetrating every inch of flesh — "

"Holmes, stop it!" I cried. It took me a moment to expunge this vivid imagery, and Holmes was gracious enough to permit me the time in silence. His fingers stopped their *rap-rap*, but his face remained grim in the moonlight.

"It is only too easy to picture Dr. Richardson performing such a horrendous act," he said, "and that worries me. Alas, we cannot draw conclusions based on one person's testimony or one's own misgivings. A good detective doesn't do that."

"Might I remind you that you're not a detective?" I scoffed, still upset.

"Perhaps I ought to consider it as a career. I am rather good at detecting—" He paused abruptly and tilted his head, ear angled towards the ceiling. "Someone is out of bed on the fir–second floor."

I craned my neck but to no avail; the house was deathly still. Not even the chirped songs of crickets disturbed the peace. I didn't bother telling Holmes that I hadn't heard anything, and I knew better than to think his imagination was overworking itself.

"Judging by the heaviness of the footsteps, I would say Mrs. H is prowling about. She really ought to consult a doctor about her insomnia." He sank back into his chair and stared out the window. "Get some sleep while you can, Watson."

"What's that supposed to mean?" I asked.

Holmes answered gravely, "A crime is under contemplation. Perhaps it has even passed this step. But we shall stop it. Sleep, Watson, sleep."

I snuggled against the pillows, feeling gloom in the place of comfort. Holmes was adept at decoding people, but I had become fairly good at reading him and all the subtle signs that accompanied his more solemn moods. I didn't like the gravity in his voice. There was also a sense of uncertainty, which was startling since the only time I had ever seen doubt on his face was when I made references to pop culture. The worst part was the dread in his tone, as though he were burdened with something cumbersome.

Or maybe my tired brain was misreading everything. This was a strong possibility, considering that Holmes rarely displayed one emotion, let alone multiple simultaneously. Still ruminating, I tossed and turned, agitated, and then finally fell into a heavy slumber.

Chapter 9 A Trail of Blood

It was all done so swiftly and deftly that the fellow was helpless before he knew that he was attacked.

—Sir Arthur Conan Doyle, *The Adventure of the Dancing Men*

"WATSON, WAKE UP!" A VOICE HISSED IN MY EAR.

Although I was convinced only minutes had passed since I had shut my eyes, Holmes had allowed me a little over four hours of sleep before this rude awakening. The night beyond the open window was still dark, but the moonlight had grown weaker. Unfortunately for shivering me, hours remained before sunlight would pour in and warm up the house since Mr. Richardson didn't seem interested in spending money on heating. Cursing the man, I pulled the comforter up to my nose and said groggily, "What do you want, Holmes?"

"I heard something."

"Feel free to elaborate whenever you're ready."

Although I couldn't make out the details of his face in the dark, there was a flash of white teeth—Holmes was grinning. "Cheeky even when you are half asleep. That is why I like you, Watson. You are full of spirit."

"Thank you for the compliment, Holmes. Now tell me what happened."

"Well, I fell asleep, although I had no intention of doing so. Two single shots of espresso are clearly too low a dosage. Better make it a double next time. Anyway, something woke me up. It sounded like a muffled bang."

"Maybe Mrs. Hudson bumped into a wall," I said, trying not to laugh.

"I doubt she has been wandering around the house for this long. I say we go investigate."

"It's probably a racoon causing a ruckus in the backyard. The city is full of them. Go back to sleep, Holmes."

There was a pause—Holmes appeared to be contemplating something. "You are not afraid, are you?"

The sneering quality of his voice irritated me. I sat up and said indignantly, "Why would I be scared?!"

"Oh, all this talk of supernatural beings...Halloween is approaching after all."

I was becoming increasingly annoyed. "So?"

"Don't you know the story behind the holiday, Watson? The Celts believed that on the night of October 31st, the boundary between the realms of the dead and the living blurs. On this day, the dead can walk among us — although it appears Dr. Richardson's ghosts have already arrived. Perhaps there was a similar Celtic holiday in September?" Holmes chuckled, but the laugh was a nervous one. He kept eyeing the door to our bedroom.

"There are no such things as ghosts," I huffed.

"Ah, but your tone sounds doubtful. We can rule out ghostly activity simply by investigating. What do you say, Watson? Oh, don't trouble yourself — stay in bed if you want."

"I'm coming," I muttered, reaching for my fleece robe.

I threw off the comforter and slid into a standing position, rubbing my eyes rigorously as I steadied my wobbly legs. The chilling air of the room made me shiver despite having put on the robe, but I swallowed my complaints and followed Holmes. There was something rather thrilling about exploring an enormous Victorian house in the dead of night.

We left the room, closing the door behind us very quietly. The hallway was dark, but my eyes adjusted to reveal a long, empty passage leading back to the foyer, which was where we found ourselves a moment later. The space was lit to some extent by the streetlamps outside, but the light that streamed in through the windows was weak and didn't quite reach the opposite wall where the staircase wound up to the second-floor landing. We had taken perhaps four or five steps into the foyer when I suddenly grabbed Holmes' arm.

"What is it?" he whispered.

"Up there." I pointed with a shaking finger at the precise spot Aurelia Richardson had stood hours before with her rope. "I saw something move up there."

"There doesn't appear to be anyone there, but humans have poor night vision and mine is no exception." He reached into the pocket of his flannel robe and pulled out something small and silver—a flashlight. If I hadn't been squinting anxiously at the landing, I may have jested that people kept smartphones rather than flashlights in their pocket. Holmes' phone, however, never seemed to be on his person, and he was constantly borrowing mine. So I supposed it was useful for him to keep a flashlight at hand, particularly for detective work in the nighttime.

The surprisingly powerful light that emanated from the tiny thing lit up the handrail and the landing beyond it quite easily. To my relief, there was nothing there. For good measure, Holmes shone the light along the length of the landing, but again we spotted nothing out of the ordinary. What had I expected to see anyway? Clearly, Mrs. Hudson's vague suggestions of spiritual activity and Aurelia's supposed entanglement with the supernatural had done a number on my already inventive brain.

"Your ghost may have wandered down the landing, Watson. Perhaps we ought to go upstairs—"

"Ghost? I didn't say ghost!" I cried indignantly, struggling to keep my voice a whisper.

"But you thought it," Holmes said, studying the rest of the foyer with his flashlight. "I don't blame you though. We've heard far too many ghost stories tod—blimey!" His light came to rest at the entrance to the hallway that led to the kitchen. There was a sharp intake of breath and then he leaped forward.

I had no idea what horrid sighting had left him speechless. The path before me was partly obscured by his wiry form, but it was the ubiquitous darkness that made much of it invisible. I half-ran to keep up and nearly collided with Holmes when he came to an abrupt stop just outside the hallway. He shone his light, and I saw his arm quiver. The gasp that escaped his lips sounded so dreadful that I pushed past him for a look. Holmes pulled me back just in time to stop me from marching into a copious, crimson pool. Illuminated by the flashlight, the contents of the hallway unraveled themselves, and I did what any sensible person would have done.

I screamed.

As I stood paralyzed, there was a cacophony of noise and movement around me. I sensed Holmes feeling the walls for a light switch as a door creaked open and muffled footsteps sounded. Within seconds, the lights came on, followed by a shrill, panicked shout and a choked exclamation.

Crucial seconds ticked by, and although I knew I couldn't afford to stand numb, there was little I could do to propel myself into action. My body seemed to only grow heavier. Holmes, on the other hand, ordered a frantic Aurora to call for an ambulance, yelled at Alejo to get hand towels, and gave me a hard shove and a hissed command, "Get a hold of yourself, Watson. Mrs. H needs us."

I wasn't convinced on that last point. The sight of Mrs. Hudson, whom I had paid little attention to back at Baker House, now filled me with a gripping terror. There was nothing I could do to help her. A masochistic voice in my head kept saying she was beyond saving, and it did indeed look like nothing short of a miracle would help. Despite the horror of it all, I couldn't peel my eyes away.

Poor Mrs. Hudson, who had been so alive just hours before, now lay lifelessly sprawled across the floor in a pool of blood. There was a red patch the size of a golf ball on the back of her head, staining her hair. Smears of blood dotted the floor and wall nearby. One slipper lay discarded not too far from where I was standing and the other dangled from her limp foot. Her body had fallen facing the opposite direction so I couldn't see her face, but that didn't stop me from imagining her blank, staring eyes. What had happened? Had the poor lady slipped and hit her head?

Alejo soon returned with the hand towels, gave some to Holmes, and then knelt and began putting pressure on the wound. With some difficulty, I dragged my attention away from Mrs. Hudson's bloodied head. But that sickening yearning for all things macabre, a sensation that plagues most of humanity, forced me to step closer. That was when I saw the wounds Holmes had started dabbing, marked by bloody slits running along the back of the nightgown. Instantly, I remembered what Holmes had said only a few hours before: *…Blow after blow penetrating every inch of flesh…* The words sounded prophetic to me now.

"Holmes," I said, trembling. "Mrs. Hudson's been m-murdered."

Even Holmes' normally pale face was deeply coloured, and his forehead shone with sweat. Yet he was calm when he responded, "Don't be ridiculous, Watson. Mrs. H is very much alive — for now. However, I agree with your point that this was a deliberate act."

His expression turned cold, but he resumed his meticulous work in silence. It was obvious that both Aurora and Alejo had heard our exchange although neither acknowledged it. Aurora remained on the phone with the dispatcher, looking worried, and the nurse was bent over his newest patient, hands working frantically to stop the bleeding. I desperately wanted to busy myself with even a menial task, but there was none at hand. Unable to stand the sight of the dying woman any longer, I left the scene. Only when I dragged my feet across the carpet and reached the staircase did I let out the breath that I had been holding. I collapsed on the step, suddenly overtaken by exhaustion.

The next few moments passed with blissful rapidity. I watched as the paramedics arrived, bringing with them a fresh burst of sounds and movements, although things were decidedly calmer now. Within minutes, they wheeled the still-breathing Mrs. Hudson out of the house, with Alejo trailing them, just as a police cruiser showed up and two officers entered the house. Luckily, they ignored me and marched straight away to the scene of the crime, where Aurora and Holmes still remained. The officers' deep voices and Aurora's high-pitched one drifted to where I sat slumped, but I had no idea what was being said. I imagined I must have looked as vacant as Aurelia—her name jolted me awake. Had she slept through the entire ordeal? I desperately hoped she had, but I had to be sure. I stood, ready to go upstairs, when someone pulled my arm roughly and jerked me backwards. Holmes, having materialized in his typical ghostly fashion, caught me in his arms and stopped my fall.

"Watson, you nearly stepped on evidence!" he exclaimed in disapproval.

Not again, I thought, and looked down. My stomach turned. There, on the second step, was a teardrop of blood. I had been sitting next to it all this time.

"Excuse me for not paying attention. I think I'm in shock," I replied weakly.

Holmes turned me around gently. I was surprised to see concern on his face. "Are you alright, Watson?"

"Never mind that. Is Mrs. Hudson going to be okay?"

"Only time will tell, but right now I think we can both use a distraction." I thought he would suggest ice cream. Instead, he said, "Let us follow this blood trail."

"What blood trail?"

"There are small specks, undoubtedly from the knife Mrs. Hudson was stabbed with, on the floor. There is a trail from the hallway leading here, so it would be reasonable to deduce that the perpetrator went up these stairs."

"But why would they do that?"

"I can think of seven reasons, but—"

"You don't think the person who did this is still upstairs, do you?" I gulped rather noticeably, but Holmes good-naturedly decided not to mock my agitation. Had we been in less funereal circumstances, he would have certainly cackled with zeal.

"That is reason number two; the perpetrator heard us as we left our rooms and dashed up the stairs to hide."

143

"Maybe that was the shadow I saw when we entered the foyer. Wait, that doesn't make sense. If he or she was standing in the hallway, st-stabbing Mrs. Hudson, then their best chance at escape would be to go down the hall, enter the kitchen, and leave through the back door."

"Good point, Watson. Why did they go upstairs? I reckon that answer could solve the case."

"Maybe they weren't familiar with the layout of the house. It could've been a robbery gone wrong."

"Hm, perhaps. Well, if you are up to it, let us proceed upstairs."

I was not a coward, but some situations demanded caution, which was not something Holmes possessed in abundance. Luckily, I was usually able to make him see reason, although that would not be the case that day. "Uh, what if the bad guy is still hiding upstairs?" I asked, nervously looking up at the black landing. "Maybe we should have the police check this out?"

"Absolutely not," Holmes said firmly. "The officers have guns; don't you think the perpetrator would feel threatened by that? What if they take Dr. Richardson as a hostage? I am confident that we can resolve this without bloodshed. We shall proceed upstairs quietly — save your clumsiness for another day, Watson — we will find Dr. Richardson and bring her downstairs, and then the police can conduct their search."

I nodded wearily, doing my best to push a vivid image of a terrifying Mr. Hyde-like creature lurking upstairs, bloody knife at the ready to silence anything that interfered with its escape. My imagination, as mentioned previously, is ruthless, and I shivered as Holmes pulled out his flashlight again. We made a slow ascent, periodically checking for blood splatters. Once, Holmes stopped abruptly in front of one such smear, remarking, "Curious!". It was smudged, unlike the others. I wondered if Alejo had unknowingly stepped on it on his way down, and my stomach turned again as I pictured what the bottom of my socks looked like.

We arrived on the landing and tiptoed down the hallway, which was lined with doors on both sides. The first door to our left was ajar; this made me stiffen nervously but prompted Holmes to take a peek. His head resurfaced a moment later.

"Mrs. H's room," he whispered matter-of-factly. Even though I had not asked for an explanation nor was I in the mood to hear one, he continued, "Very obviously a guest room. Minimal furnishings and virtually no personal items. The lamp is still on, and there is a book on the bed. When we—I—heard her prowling the house earlier, she was clearly making her way to the library, looking for something to read. It

145

looks like she found a book and brought it up here."

I sighed. "If only she had stayed in bed."

We turned our attention to the door on our right, which also stood open. This time, Holmes strode in, waving his flashlight. I followed reluctantly but remained alert.

"The nurse's room," Holmes said quietly, scanning the surroundings.

The room was lit only by the weak moonlight that streamed through the gossamer-like curtains. Holmes put away his flashlight and turned on the lights, which brought to sight a bed that had obviously been slept in, a chest of drawers, and a bedside table stacked with a few books. The clothes Alejo had worn that day lay on a chair—the obvious clue that had led Holmes to his deduction.

"Also, the books are in Tagalog, Alejo's native tongue," Holmes offered, and started chuckling when he saw my expression of incredulity. "Oh, don't give me that look."

"Stop reading my mind," I hissed, fully aware of the absurdity of my statement.

"You know very well that mind reading is impossible. It was quite apparent what you were thinking when your eyes came to rest on the clothes—a slight rolling up of the eyes and a nearly imperceptible nod of the head, as though you had come to a sudden realization. Quite apparent, you see. Hm, perhaps you *are* in shock. Watson, I thought you were made of

146

tougher stuff." Again, there was that infuriating chuckle.

After all that had happened, I could scarcely be blamed for the blinding anger that overtook me without warning. My fears of a knife-wielding assailant lurking nearby vanished — for a few seconds — and I roared like a fool, "We can't all be robots, Sherlock Holmes! Normal people get emotional when someone they know is nearly murdered."

An uncomfortable silence impregnated the room, and soon thereafter, my unease returned. I reprimanded myself severely for the outburst, picturing the silver glint of our impending demise. Then, I contemplated Holmes' response. Strangely, his reaction made me more nervous than the unseen danger and I braced myself. I expected words of a tempestuous nature, or perhaps subdued nonchalance if his mind was otherwise preoccupied, as was the case at that moment. However, when he spoke, his tone was gentle.

"I apologize, Watson," he said. "I know that it hasn't been an easy night. What you witnessed today will stay with you for a long time, and I am at fault for bringing you here. I would have never involved you if I had known."

This rare moment of compassion was followed by an awkward silence. Any anger that remained on my part dissipated, and I cleared my throat and mumbled, "No apology necessary, friend."

Holmes, content once again, proceeded towards the object that had captured his interest just moments before my outpouring. Fortunately, it was neither the perpetrator's hiding spot nor another gruesome blood stain. It was a door that I had initially assumed led to a closet.

"What's behind the door?" I asked.

"Dr. Richardson's room, of course. You may recall Roksanda mentioning that Dr. Richardson's room is connected to Alejo's? No? Ah, well. Onwards then."

The door was opened quietly, and we entered to find another furnished room, much of it resembling the one we had left behind although it was more spacious and opulent. There was a large portable heater, a sofa, a wooden coffee table, a floor lamp, and a bookcase that extended along the length of one wall, similar to Holmes' one at Baker House. The shelves had not been sufficient enough to house Aurelia's books though; there were quite a few volumes sitting on the floor and even a handful on her bed, where her still form slept.

The moonlight, which entered through a pair of French doors that led to a small balcony, and the light that streamed in from Alejo's room allowed us to see that there was no one but the intended occupant. Apart from the closet, there were no other hiding places, but my unease persisted until Holmes opened the closet door and shone his flashlight around. Luckily, it was devoid of intruders, and we returned our attention to the sleeping Aurelia.

Holmes turned on the floor lamp. I would have preferred to remain in the dark, for there was something protective about it. Perhaps this was my intuition's way of delaying the unfortunate scene that awaited us. Being the sharp-witted person he was, Holmes processed it faster than I did; he whirled around, index finger at his lips, eyes desperately commanding me not to make a sound. But it was too late. The shock of what lay on the bed shook me and I gasped loudly.

Chapter 10 The Hand that Dealt the Blow

"You can take my word that she is innocent."
—Sir Arthur Conan Doyle, *The Crooked Man*

THE PICTURE OF A SICKLY WOMAN SLEEPING soundly may have induced melancholy in an observer, maybe even serenity when one saw her long, ebony hair, moonlit skin, and frail body wrapped in a rose-coloured nightgown. Despite the chill in the room, Aurelia had not covered herself with a sheet. Her hands rested on her belly in a corpse-like manner, but she was very much alive. Her chest went up and down rhythmically, and the knife that one hand clasped, its blade nestled between her breasts, followed suit. It was streaked with blood, and the nightgown beneath it had turned from pink to red.

I immediately distanced myself from the bed. Unfortunately, my step back landed on a pile of books on the floor, and I lost my balance and fell with a violent thud.

Aurelia stirred.

I looked up at Holmes, panicked. Again, he put a finger to his lips. As I did my best not to fidget, he tiptoed to the foot of the bed and knelt to examine the still sleeping woman's socked feet. The examination took no longer than ten seconds. He then straightened and called out Aurelia's name loudly — much to my horror.

Aurelia stirred once more before her eyes opened. She blinked and then blinked again. Finally, she sat up and stared at Holmes. Perhaps it had been the weight of the knife, or maybe it was the wetness of her nightgown that caused her to look down at the object in her hand. At first, there was surprise on her face — which baffled me. Had she forgotten what she had done? Was she really surprised by the knife or was she feigning to trick us? Another part of me wondered why a murderer would sleep with the murder weapon at hand. Had the weapon been planted? The answer to this last question arrived an instant later when Aurelia's initial surprise disappeared, replaced abruptly by recognition. Lost between sobs, her voice was barely audible, but I caught the following:

"No, no, not again. Not again."

She had sprung out of the bed, knife still at hand, before I could even comprehend the meaning of her words. Holmes stepped out of her way hastily, and she ran past us, simultaneously crying and calling out incoherently.

We trailed her as she ran out the door like a madwoman, stopping only once when she paused to look up and down the hallway. Apparently not seeing what she was looking for, she sprinted down the stairs, still wielding the knife. Her anxiety only grew when she reached the foyer; the voices of the police and her sister pulled her to the hallway. Standing some distance behind her, I could only imagine what her face must have looked like at the sight of the blood. Whereas it had shocked me into stillness, it propelled Aurelia forward, hungry for a closer look. This never came to pass though since both officers drew out their guns.

For one long minute, the house was frozen in utter terror. Aurelia stared, her agitated movements finally stiffening when she saw the officers standing poised, guns pointed, voices commanding, and eyes watchful. Aurora sobbed loudly and begged her sister to drop the knife, but the distraught woman did no such thing. She remained still, but I could see her large eyes darting back and forth between the guns and the blood as Holmes pulled me to the wall to get us out of the line of fire. For the second time that night, I stood paralyzed, this time in awful anticipation.

"Dr. Richardson," interjected a soft voice. "You need to put the knife down. Ruth is in the hospital now, but she will be alright." It was Holmes and he managed to silence both the officers and Aurora with this statement. Aurelia, on the other hand, finally spoke.

"No, Sherlock Holmes, Ruth is dead. Martha is in the hospital."

She let the knife drop, and as it hit the carpet with a muffled clank, something pivotal seemed to drain from her body. Her shoulders slumped, her head bowed in shame, and her hands covered her face as she cried silently. The police reached her before Aurora could, and although the younger tried to reach out for the elder, Aurelia was steered out the front door as soon as her rights had been recited. Aurora followed them, wailing even more loudly than her sister.

The door banged shut, and I fell back against the wall and slid down, watching the bursts of red and blue police car lights that entered the foyer through the windows. I grew more miserable with every flash. Holmes knelt and stared at me intently.

"Watson, I need you to focus. I know this has been a terrible ordeal, but if Mrs. H finds out I let Dr. Richardson go to prison for a crime she didn't commit, she will either murder me or never speak to me again. Neither circumstance is ideal, so get up. We need to get to the bottom of this."

I stood unsteadily. "Did you just say Aurelia didn't commit—"

"Well, obviously. That's quite apparent. Being in shock is no excuse for not paying attention to one's sur—hm, perhaps I am being a bit unsympathetic—"

"Holmes!"

"Alright, no need for raised tones." He took a swift breath. "Three clues point to Dr. Richardson's innocence. First, her look of surprise when she woke up and saw the knife. Second, she had no idea where to find the victim. Note how she stepped into the hallway and didn't know which way to turn. Only when she heard voices from downstairs did she go in that direction."

"What if she had one of her episodes and then forgot what she did? That would explain both of those things," I interjected.

Holmes nodded approvingly. "Watson, you are rather excellent at playing devil's advocate. Your theory is certainly a possibility, but there is more to this story than meets the eye, such as the third clue—the lack of blood on her socks. There was smeared blood on the 14th step, which I believe the perpetrator stepped on. Those specks of blood are quite suggestive actually, but more on that later. Now, where was I? Oh, yes, the blood on the step—Dr. Richardson's socks were clean."

"Maybe she put on a clean pair."

"I plan on carrying out a search of her room to verify that, although I do not think that will be necessary. Alas, it is best not to leave any stone unturned." That last bit was said quietly, and I felt the change in tone implied there was more to it. I didn't question it, however. Instead, I voiced my own suspicion. "I thought maybe Alejo had stepped on it on his way down."

But Holmes shook his head. "Not a chance. He was wearing slippers with a rubber sole, which are not very absorbent. Someone wearing socks stepped on the blood, and the material absorbed the majority of it, leaving behind only a sliver of blood. But you are right on one account, Watson."

I waited for an explanation, for once my curiosity too exhausted to probe and pry.

"Someone stepped on the blood descending the stairs, not ascending. That is quite apparent from the direction of the smear. Yes, I know that sounds strange, but it fits perfectly with my theory. Someone went upstairs with the intention of placing the knife in Dr. Richardson's room and then accidentally stepped on the blood on their way downstairs."

"Why would someone frame Aurelia?"

"Because it is believable. She has a history of erratic behaviour and has been institutionalized. People won't have a hard time believing she hurt Mrs. H, which will allow the culprit to get away with it."

"But Aurelia knew Mrs. Hudson had been hurt. How could she know that if she'd been asleep the whole time?

"Because she is observant." Holmes paused as if waiting for me to make the realization that he no doubt had made long ago. No such epiphany arose, however, so I remained silent. After a sigh, he continued, "There were six people in the house. When Dr. Richardson arrived in the foyer and saw the blood in the hallway, there were two missing, Mrs. H and Alejo. It was apparent to her one of them had been hurt. So how did she know which one?"

"Holmes, I'm too tired for your games. Just tell me."

"Oh, alright. The slippers, Watson. She could see Mrs. H's slippers from her vantage point. It was lying there amidst the blood, making it quite apparent who the victim is. Now, enough chitchat. I estimate we have ten minutes before the forensics unit arrives. We should begin our investigation before they muddle the crime scene like a herd of buffaloes."

I scoffed. "Do you really think you're better than the professionals?" For this impertinent comment, I received an arresting glare.

"I have a knack for seeing what others don't. Do you deny that?"

I opted for silence since my answer would have only further inflated his ego. Regardless, Holmes smiled in a self-satisfied way as he walked to the front door. But by the time he opened it and peeked outside, his face looked grim again. Widening the gap, he knelt and examined the lock.

"One officer parked in front of the house," he murmured, "but he appears quite relaxed since he thinks the attacker is safely in cuffs. I reckon he won't even notice me."

My limbs twitched nervously anyway as I watched the cruiser through the gate. Nearly two minutes later, Holmes straightened, apparently finding nothing of interest, and strode down the hallway. Thankful that we weren't stopping there, I followed, carefully dodging the blood. We entered the kitchen, turned on the lights, and reached the patio door. Holmes barked at me once for blocking the light as he conducted his examination of the lock on that door but remained silent afterwards. This time, he took no longer than a minute. Closing the door, through which a horrendously chilling air was flowing in, he looked at my shivering form disapprovingly and then glanced around. He surveyed everything in sight before muttering, "Well, well, what is that?"

Kneeling by the door, he stared at the ground for a moment before picking up a spot of dirt and bringing it close to one eye. "Have a gander at this, Watson. Do you recall seeing a pair of shoes here earlier?"

I shook my head, peering at the speck of brown that rested on his long index finger.

"Is that soil from the yard?" I asked.

"It certainly seems so. There is also a faint, incomplete outline of shoes here. Impossible to see any distinguishing features or determine size, unfortunately, but most suggestive nonetheless."

"And what exactly does it suggest?"

Instead of answering, he shook his head impatiently. "There is no time for discussion. If you will follow me."

Annoyed though I was, I obliged. Much to my chagrin, Holmes' investigation lay in the hallway this time. Although I knew this would happen eventually, I couldn't help but feel squeamish. My mind's involuntary projections of the old housekeeper still lying in a pool of her own blood didn't help matters. I shook my head and prayed that the wave of nausea would pass. My friend, on the other hand, had a spark in his eyes, like a hound on the trail of a fresh scent. I noticed he was eyeing the blood that was splattered on the wall with interest.

Clearing my throat to push down the bile that was snaking its way up, I grumbled, "Feel free to think out loud. It'll be the only way I get to find out what's going on."

Holmes answered first with a steely gaze; his unblinking, grey eyes were nearly as unnerving as the blood on the wall. "That blood," he finally said, pointing to the wall, "is the result of the head injury. Someone pushed Mrs. H and she hit her head. What we see on the floor was due to the stab wounds. My question is why here? Why this particular hallway?"

"Maybe the perp was walking down the hallway when Mrs. Hudson surprised him."

"I don't think Mrs. H is capable of surprising anyone. I have seen her descend the stairs at Baker House, huffing and puffing for breath. The lady has zero stamina. Thus, if she came down from the second floor, her wheezing would have alerted the culprit. Furthermore, her being a heavyset woman and the plastic soles of her slippers being quite loud, there would have been ample notice. The perpetrator could have run back into the kitchen or even into the yard to avoid detection."

"And yet they didn't."

Holmes looked thoughtful. "Perhaps they couldn't." He whirled around to face the opposite wall, his nose only inches away from the wallpaper as he inspected each painting on display. Finally, he pulled away, looking as grim as some of the portraits of the Richardson ancestors. Something had obviously caught his attention, but I knew he would keep the detail to himself unless I intervened with an observation of my own.

"Aurelia's painting is crooked," I pointed out. "I'm pretty sure it wasn't like that before."

"I don't think Dr. Richardson will appreciate you calling it her painting, but yes, you are correct. How do you suppose that happened?"

159

"There was obviously a struggle. Maybe Mrs. Hudson pushed the perp, and they fell against the painting."

"Brilliant, Watson!"

With another sudden twirl, he exited the hallway, crossed the foyer, and strode up the stairs just as sirens sounded in the distance. They grew loud very quickly, but by that point, we were already in Aurelia's room, and Holmes had started rummaging through her things. Once he finished, he opened the French doors and entered the balcony. I curiously watched him study the ground with his flashlight; he knelt and appeared to pick up something although I could see nothing in his hand. My attention soon drifted to the bed, and I felt a chill—unrelated to the one that seeped in through the open doors—as I recalled the sight of a ghostly woman sleeping with a glimmering blade. Downstairs, I could hear the shuffling of feet and muffled voices.

"There is nothing here that ties Dr. Richardson to Mrs. H's assault," Holmes declared once he returned.

"Except for the bloody knife, of course," I responded sarcastically.

"That was obviously planted. Haven't I convinced you of that yet? No? Well, all in good time."

Holmes' confidence was encouraging, but as I glanced around Aurelia's room, a fresh wave of melancholy overtook me. "I don't understand why any of this happened."

My friend nodded sympathetically. "As a rule, the bigger the crime, the more obvious the motive. But in this case, I am utterly perplexed. We should go downstairs now. The detective inspector in charge will want to question us. Let us keep our theories to ourselves, agreed?"

Wearily, I followed him out of the room.

*

The interrogation lasted no more than half an hour. The story we disclosed to the police was that I, a friend of the family—not an amateur investigator of paranormal or other happenings—had awoken in the middle of the night, thirsty, and had found Mrs. Hudson on my way to the kitchen. My scream had woken the rest of the household—this part, at least, was true.

Despite the frantic state of my mind, exhaustion overwhelmed the body, and I managed to sleep for two hours. I woke up to a crackling fire, my body curled to fit in the loveseat of the library. Holmes sat adjacent to me in the armchair; he was staring into the fireplace as though entranced by the dancing flames.

"Holmes," I said softly. "Did you get any sleep?"

"Of course not," he answered, although this was already obvious from the bags that lingered beneath his hooded eyelids.

"What time is it? Did I miss anything? Where is everyone?"

"It is a little after seven o'clock. Mr. Richardson is on his way home from Milan and is due to arrive around two pm. Roksanda should have already arrived but appears to be running late. She has yet to be informed of what has happened. Mrs. H was still in critical condition when I called the hospital half an hour ago, and Aurora, if my hearing is accurate, is walking down the hallway, most likely coming to see us."

A moment later, a weary-looking Aurora stepped into the library, walked sluggishly over to where we sat, and slumped down next to me. The sight of her was shocking; lack of sleep (and her customary splash of vibrant makeup) had transformed her into something gaunt and lifeless. Like Holmes, there were noticeable bags underneath her eyes, but whereas his eyes shone with fervor, hers looked moist and red. Her whole body, including her large belly, sagged as though she were barely able to sit up straight.

"Are you okay, Aurora?" I asked.

"That's the stupidest thing anyone's asked me today," she cried. "Do I look okay? I look horrible. Not a wink of sleep. This is going to be terrible for my complexion." She pulled at her cheek and groaned.

"Watson was referring to how you feel about your sister's incarceration," Holmes said stiffly.

Aurora's face darkened and she scowled. "When this gets out, I think I'm going to die of humiliation."

"That would be a loss indeed."

The sarcasm in Holmes' tone was obvious, but either Aurora chose to ignore it or she was too emotionally preoccupied to notice. Holmes looked vaguely annoyed, a sentiment that I shared as well. Aurora had suddenly crept onto my suspect list, although why she would want to hurt the old housekeeper was beyond me. Perhaps her goal had been to hurt her sister, and poor Mrs. Hudson had been a means to accomplishing that. Suspicious though I was, I couldn't wholeheartedly convince myself that Aurora was the culprit. She had seemed genuinely distressed during her sister's arrest and had even been opposed to having her institutionalized again. Yet she had transformed into a rather ugly thing over the course of a few hours. The woman was a puzzle.

"Does that mean you believe Aurelia stabbed Mrs. Hudson?" I asked.

Aurora looked at me as though I couldn't possibly say anything more stupid — apart from my first question, of course. "The knife was in her hand. Isn't it obvious? Considering her past, it's —" Here, her mouth clamped shut, and I immediately knew she had said far more than she had wanted to. Much to my surprise, Holmes remained quiet, his curiosity not even the least bit aroused. I, however, wasn't going to let the opportunity slip.

"What past? Has Aurelia hurt someone before? Is that why she was sent away? Was it her colleague, Ruth?"

For once, Aurora looked intimidated, for I had struck a nerve. Her reaction convinced me that Aurelia had done something terrible in her past, something connected to her breakdown. Perhaps there had been truth to her confession in the library. Mrs. Hudson either hadn't known the details or had simply lied to Holmes. I was preparing another torrent of questions when Holmes interjected.

"Watson, where are your manners! Dr. Richardson's past is personal information, and you are not entitled to it." He shot a quick look at his watch and then turned to Aurora, his initial expression of annoyance now replaced with sympathy. "I apologize for my friend's impertinence."

I took this as a sign to remain quiet; Holmes either had no interest in Aurelia's (possible) criminal past because it was nonexistent or had no bearing on the case…or he had initiated some scheme. But if he thought tact was the best way to compel headstrong Aurora into divulging the details we so craved, he was wrong. There was obvious relief on the woman's face, and her lips remained stubbornly shut.

"Is there even the remotest of possibilities that Mrs. H was caught up in a robbery gone wrong?" Holmes asked delicately. "Perhaps the security system caught some funny business?"

But Aurora shook her head. "Oh, eh, well, dad cancelled the service weeks ago. He doesn't think — well, he — "

"I am not surprised. Putting up a sign is considerably cheaper than a real security system. Mr. Richardson doesn't seem to think heating the house is a worthy investment either. Poor Watson nearly froze to death last night. I hope he is not facing any financial troubles?"

Aurora blushed. "Oh, no. Dad's always been like this. He grew up poor so — "

"Ah, I see. Anyway, have you been to the hospital? Did you see Mrs. H?"

"I went there straight after the police station. They wouldn't let me see her, but the doctors said — "

"Yes, yes, I've already spoken to the doctors," Holmes interrupted. "Now tell me, did you see Alejo there?"

Aurora blinked. "Um, now that you mention it, no. I was there for close to an hour, and I didn't see him anywhere."

Strangely, Holmes didn't seem surprised by this news.

"Maybe he went home," I suggested.

"This is his home. He's a live-in nurse," Aurora said. "I don't think he has family here; he's never mentioned anyone, but I guess he also doesn't talk much."

"I presume you have his mobile number?" Holmes asked. "Kindly give him a call and find out his whereabouts." His voice was calm, but there was an excited twinkle in his eyes that even Aurora noticed. She cast me a quizzical look; the crinkling of her nose plainly conveyed her displeasure at sharing the space with an oddball like Holmes. Nevertheless, she pulled out a large smartphone from the pocket of her jeans and began fumbling with it.

We waited in silence. Something was on the verge of unfolding—that was easily detectable from the impatient way Holmes' long fingers drummed against the armrest—but I had no idea what.

"No answer," Aurora finally said. "Um, should I be concerned?"

"I think not. I was simply confirming something." In one swift motion, Holmes stood up and prompted me to follow suit. "I believe the front door just opened. Poor Roksanda must be in a state of shock, seeing the police tape." His face didn't look sympathetic in the least though. When Aurora stood, he motioned her to sit. "Oh, you should stay here and get some rest. You look absolutely dreadful. We shall fill her in and possibly persuade her to make breakfast. I am simply famished!"

Chapter 11 A Criminal Past

"The past and the present are within the field of my inquiry…"

—Sir Arthur Conan Doyle, *The Hound of the Baskervilles*

W E FOUND THE YOUNG HOUSEKEEPER STANDING by the yellow tape the police had pinned around the entrance to the hallway. She was dressed in a fur-trimmed, quilted, red parka and matching hat, looking as though she were about to embark on an Arctic expedition. Hearing our footsteps, she whirled around with bulging eyes and a gaping mouth.

"What hap—" she began.

"Mrs. H was attacked early this morning," Holmes began, "stabbed multiple times in that hallway. She has been taken to the hospital and remains in critical condition. Dr. Richardson has been arrested for the crime." He then launched into a brief retelling of how we had found the knife.

Roksanda's mortification rendered her too stunned to speak. Although she tried her best not to survey the hallway, her eyes jumped back to the scene of the crime against her will. My eyes followed suit, and I shuddered when I saw the blood again. Roksanda finally overcame her internal struggles and looked away, blinking rapidly. I hoped she wouldn't burst into tears; seeing teary-eyed people always made my eyes water.

"Why didn't Mr. Richardson just listen to me?" she lamented, finally having found her voice. "Aurelia hasn't been doing well for weeks now, but he wouldn't admit it. I tried speaking to him about it; he wouldn't listen. But even I didn't think something like this would happen."

"Yes, it is quite shocking," Holmes said, although his tone conveyed no such emotion. Instead, he licked his lips, his gaze extending past the atrocities of the hallway. I was astonished to see that his focus lingered on the kitchen entrance. Was he actually thinking about food at a time like this? Admittedly, my tired body ached for some coffee, but I had enough tact to not voice this out loud. Holmes, on the other hand, expressed tact only when it suited him to do so.

"I presume the only way to the kitchen now is through the back door?" he asked a still-stunned Roksanda. It seemed she had temporarily forgotten the layout of the house; her eyes travelled to the hallway once again, and for a long moment, she didn't respond, her mind preoccupied with no doubt sombre thoughts.

"Yeah, the back door," came her meek reply at last.

"Excellent," Holmes said with gusto. "Thirty seconds of fresh air will be invigorating. Watson certainly needs it; she looks knackered. Strong coffee will help as well. Shall we proceed?"

Before the housekeeper could question or protest this, Holmes slid his arm around hers and propelled her out the front door. Anticipating the morning chill, I adjusted my robe tightly around my body and then ran after them. We cut through the messy lawn, passing by the garage, to a stone pathway that led to the backyard. Dead leaves littered our path, and the ones that remained on the trees swayed precariously in the gentle morning breeze. Apart from this rustling, the neighbourhood was silent. I longed to see movement — a stray cat, a school bus full of noisy children, a suavely dressed businessman climbing into a sports car — any sign of life would have sufficed. My plea, however, went unanswered and all remained still. I continued my march sullenly, even though the crisp air was waking me up faster than coffee could.

Before long, Holmes and I were seated on bar stools, watching Roksanda, who, after discarding her coat and purse, looked around the kitchen as though she had no idea what she ought to be doing. Seeing the sliding doors, beyond which lay the dreaded hallway, incited a sense of purpose in her, and she practically ran to close them. Her relief was obvious, as was mine. It almost felt like an ordinary Monday morning, although I didn't ordinarily spend any morning sitting in the pristine kitchen of a multi-million-dollar home.

"If you can make a pot of coffee, we would be most grateful," Holmes said. I wholeheartedly agreed, although I was far too bashful to say so. Apparently, my friend had not finished ordering his breakfast, for he continued, "And perhaps some hard-boiled eggs? Just two will do for me, along with some buttered toast."

Roksanda looked startled at first, but perhaps happy for the distraction, she began preparing the coffee without a rebuttal. Ten minutes later, after two steaming mugs had been placed before us, she spoke. "I don't know if I should even be here. With more than half the family gone, I—"

"Food is of utmost importance for a family in distress," Holmes interrupted. "I believe Aurora hasn't eaten anything since last night, and the Richardsons will surely want some nourishment when they arrive in a couple of hours. You must be here to take care of the house and the family, Roksanda."

If the speech had been meant to uplift spirits and provoke a sense of self-importance, it worked. Roksanda straightened a bit, nodded in acquiescence, and began preparing Holmes' breakfast. She compelled me to eat as well, but I politely refused, my appetite not yet fully restored. As Holmes' eggs boiled, she began making an omelette, presumably for Aurora.

"So when did you two get here? Did Aurora call you?" she asked.

"The answer to that lies in front of you. You must simply observe," my friend responded ominously.

I personally thought a concise response detailing our invitation to spend the night would have been the best answer, considering the circumstances. Roksanda appeared to be in no mood to play Holmes' game, and her scowl prompted him to answer.

"We are in our pyjamas as you can see," he said, pointing at my robe. "We spent the night here at Mrs. H's request."

"Oh, I didn't know anything about that. Why did she invite you both to stay? Did something happen in the evening?"

"No, nothing out of the ordinary happened," Holmes said. "I suppose with Mr. and Mrs. Richardson gone, there would only be three people in the house and that unnerved Mrs. H. I am not exactly a supporter of intuition, but for some reason, she felt uneasy and thought more bodies in the house was better."

"Are you saying Martha knew something was going to happen?" Roksanda asked.

"Perhaps," Holmes answered. "Perhaps even you knew something was going to happen."

This perked my attention, and I put my coffee down. "What's that supposed to mean?" Judging by the housekeeper's face, she was wondering the same thing. The response that came failed to provide any meaningful answers though.

"I know all about it, Roksanda. Mrs. H told me," Holmes said quietly.

The housekeeper's grimace deepened. "What are you talking about?"

"About Dr. Richardson."

Roksanda's shoulders slumped. For a moment, she didn't say anything, opting to fumble with the omelette instead. What astonished me was the expression on Holmes' face; it was jubilant, as though he had been knighted for some marvelous achievement. I wondered if he was referring to Aurelia's past and the reason she had been institutionalized. Why he would be open to discussing the matter with Roksanda rather than Aurora confounded me, but I stayed quiet and watchful.

"I didn't know Martha was aware of what happened to Aurelia. The family is very close-lipped about personal things. It's nothing to gossip about." She shot a cold glance in my direction, and I did my best to look affronted, even though I was desperate to know more.

"Mrs. H trusts me completely, which is why she told me, and I can vouch for Watson. She will not breathe a word. You can speak freely in front of her," Holmes said.

Roksanda didn't look convinced. She eyed me suspiciously, although I had no idea what I had done to deserve this level of scrutiny.

"Watson and I have been traumatized by Mrs. H's attack." Holmes turned solemnly to face me. "I am very sorry for putting you through this. Like Mr. Richardson, I never thought something like this would happen—that the past would repeat itself."

I did my best to look traumatized, although very little acting was required. I must have looked as wretched as I felt, for my hair was unkempt, my pajamas were wrinkled, and my face was dry and unwashed. But beyond the fatigue and shock, I possessed enough acuity to detect something ingenuine about Holmes' apology. My friend was a first-rate actor, and he had fooled me a handful of times in the last few weeks, but this time, with that morning's sincere apology still fresh on my mind, I had a standard to compare it to. The performance was more or less convincing, and yet it appeared staged.

"Watson has every right to know why all this happened. If you can tell the story…" his voice trailed.

Again, the housekeeper looked hesitant, but after a moment, she sighed. "I guess I can do that. First of all, you didn't hear any of this from me. The family didn't tell me anything. I—uh— overheard Mr. Richardson talking about it on the phone to his sister a few days after Aurelia arrived. Up until that point, I had no idea she'd been institutionalized. She was mentioned in passing, and when I asked Martha about her, she said Aurelia was an archaeologist and was living abroad."

Luckily, we were spared the "anthropologist" correction; although Holmes had opened his mouth, he managed to stifle the temptation and allowed the housekeeper to go on with her tale.

"One day in January," Roksanda began, "Mr. Richardson brought Aurelia home, with no warning at all. Mrs. Richardson was furious at first, but Aurelia kept to herself and didn't bother anyone. Alejo was hired to take care of her, and everything was almost back to normal. But even before the nurse came along, I could tell there was something odd about her, and I suspected she'd been hospitalized all that time. I was curious, but I knew my place, and I knew it was none of my business so I didn't pry. Then, I overheard the phone call, and I haven't been able to look at Aurelia in the same way, even though I know it wasn't her fault. She didn't mean to and—"

Holmes cleared his throat loudly. "If you can recite just the facts? I believe Watson will need to leave soon for her nine o'clock science fiction class—a complete waste of a course if you ask me, but literary types are seldom attracted to practical subjects."

I glared at him. "Like chemistry?"

"Exactly. Why do we need science fiction when life is infinitely stranger? I don't understand how you stomach fiction with all of its conventionalities and predictable conclusions. You really ought to consider medicine. It would help me immensely. Interesting though the subject is, it is taking up far too much space in my brain attic…"

He rambled on for another minute or so in this fashion, although his arguments failed to convince me. I was, however, thankful for the reminder since it had escaped my mind that Monday meant a return to classes. Three hours of readings and riveting discussion were exactly what I needed to distract myself. I wondered if Holmes would attend his classes today; something told me the matter at hand took precedence over organic chemistry despite it being a very "practical" subject.

Finally, Holmes returned his attention to Roksanda and prompted her to continue.

"Fine, I'll tell you what I overheard, but don't judge me too harshly for being nosy." We nodded, and she continued, "Six years ago, Aurelia was in a bad state. Her husband left her. That's when the drinking started. She lost custody of her daughter because of this. She would've lost her job too if Mr. Richardson hadn't intervened by financing a small excavation on some island near Africa to—" Roksanda's nose crinkled "—dig up bones."

Holmes, on the other hand, nodded ardently. "I've read some papers Dr. Richardson has written on our early human ancestors. A fascinating topic! Did Mr. Richardson ever mention the name of this island?"

Roksanda didn't seem as captivated by the prospect of uncovering human remains, albeit ancient ones. In fact, she looked mildly appalled but kept quiet about her feelings in the midst of Holmes' enthusiasm. "Uh, I think he said it was near Cape Town."

"Hm, there is one, but I doubt it was where Dr. Richardson went. It was once a prison for political prisoners, such as Nelson Mandela, and is now a museum. I had the pleasure of touring the prison earlier this year. The guide was an ex-inmate and was able to provide firsthand experiences of what prison life was like. See, Watson, I was learning without university." Holmes had the glazed look of someone reliving a pleasant memory, and I guessed he was referring to how he had spent the days following his expulsion. "Excuse the digression," he said. "Dr. Richardson's destination should be easy enough to uncover, if needed. Go on with your narrative, please."

The housekeeper took a moment to check on the eggs, but unable to delay any longer without making her reluctance obvious, she spoke. "The excavation party was small. Aurelia and her colleague, Ruth, supervised the dig, and their three graduate students were also there."

"Their names, if you please."

"Uh, Michael, Caleb, and Linda, if I'm remembering correctly. I don't know their last names."

"Excellent," Holmes said. "Carry on."

"At first, the dig did exactly what Mr. Richardson hoped it would do. It was a good distraction, but I don't think Aurelia would've gone mad if she'd stayed home. The stories she heard from the locals, the intense heat, and maybe even withdrawal symptoms—I think that's what made her snap."

"Ah, but had she stayed here, her liver would have likely disintegrated, and Mr. Richardson would only have one daughter left."

Roksanda opened her mouth to say something but stopped quickly. Had she been about to say that that would have been a better alternative?

"What stories did she hear?" I asked, wondering how a story could drive someone mad.

"Well, people had apparently gone missing throughout the years on the island. The locals blamed the cannibals who lived in the woods." Roksanda's eyes shone with excitement even though she tried to keep her tone nonchalant. "Whether these people exist or not, I don't know, but Aurelia's team was forbidden from entering the woods, even though it was quicker to cut through it when going back to the village from the dig site."

"Alas, curiosity prevailed and they disobeyed," Holmes said quietly.

The housekeeper nodded. "The locals also spoke of the Place. There's no specific name; everyone just called it the Place. Either it was where people went to die, or people were lured there by forces unknown to die—I'm not sure exactly what it is. Aurelia mentions it from time to time, but she's always very cryptic."

"Do you recall anything she has said about it? For example, has she described what it looks like?" Holmes asked.

Roksanda shrugged. "I don't really remember. I think once she referred to it as a place of punishment. Anyway, one day, the team cut through the woods, and not everyone came back out."

It was the worst time for a pause, but that is exactly what the housekeeper did. I had held my breath, afraid of blurting out a question and causing a digression, although it was Holmes who had been doing that throughout the conversation. Unfortunately, it seemed no excuse was needed to trigger reticence in Roksanda. Her lips clamped shut in refusal to utter another word. This made my sense of foreboding worsen. I could already picture how the tale would end, and it was *not* pleasant.

"So what happened?" I asked, unable to bear the silence.

The answer didn't come right away, but the housekeeper eventually summoned the courage to talk. "Aurelia started hallucinating. She thought she was being dragged off to the Place. She thought she was being punished for the alcoholism, for not being a good mother, and she just went nuts and killed everyone." The last bit was uttered in such haste that I looked at Holmes with incredulity, doubting if I had heard correctly. His expression, unfortunately, told me that my hearing was in perfect working condition. Nevertheless, it was difficult to picture the dainty and child-like Aurelia Richardson slaying four people, her mind taunted by a distorted reality. The imagining was oxymoronic to say the least, and I wasn't sure I believed it. But Roksanda seemed genuinely perturbed by the retelling; she stared, dazed, at nothing in particular, and her fingers twitched involuntarily. I had no choice but to believe.

"Oh dear," Holmes murmured. "I presume the victims were stabbed to death?"

"How did you know that?" The surprised housekeeper didn't receive a verbal answer; a nonchalant shrug and a wave of the hand were all she got.

"It was just a guess," I said. "Right, Holmes?"

Holmes looked veritably appalled by this. "I never guess. It is a shocking habit — destructive to the logical faculty." Roksanda and I exchanged a glance that went unnoticed. After a pensive silence, he continued, "Was Dr. Richardson in the habit of carrying a knife?"

Roksanda shrugged. "I have no idea. I don't know where she got the knife from. Maybe it was a souvenir? Maybe she bought it for protection against the cannibals. You know, I asked Martha about Aurelia's past a few weeks after she moved in. It didn't seem as though she knew anything about what happened."

"That attests to her character, doesn't it? She can be trusted to keep secrets," Holmes replied, and the housekeeper reddened.

"Look, I only told you because—"

"You have nothing to be apologetic about. In fact, you have been very helpful. We shall now try to put this dreadful story out of our minds. I believe the eggs are ready?"

I was sure Roksanda was as shocked as I was by Holmes' appetite at so troublesome a time; we both glared at him disapprovingly. As Roksanda resumed her work, juggling food and plates, Holmes watched her as though nothing could be more mesmeric. I, on the other hand, fidgeted restlessly in my seat. A plate of eggs and toast was soon placed before Holmes.

"I'll go give this to Aurora now," Roksanda said, picking up another plate of food. She left hurriedly as though afraid that Holmes would continue the conversation. She was clearly done talking and would remain stubbornly reserved if the topic of Aurelia's past was approached again.

I turned to Holmes, who was chewing his buttered toast with relish. "Maybe this is why

Aurelia looks so sad all the time. She feels guilty about what she did."

"I am inclined to agree. It is a terrible burden to bear."

"I guess that's why she decided to unload some of it yesterday."

"Ah, but Dr. Richardson doesn't seem to have the need to confess. Except for vague snippets here and there, she hadn't confessed in all these months to her family or to the woman who raised her. But you, Watson—you incited a confession. It is rather fortunate you resemble her graduate student—the one she killed."

"I—what? But Roksanda said her name was Linda."

"Sounds quite similar to the name Dr. Richardson mentioned yesterday, wouldn't you say? Ka-lin-da." Holmes enunciated the name slowly, as though savouring it, before swallowing a large forkful of eggs. Chewing did *not* impede his ability to talk, and I got an eyeful of the squishy, yellow contents of his mouth. "Roksanda either misremembered the name or misheard."

At the time, I too had regarded the resemblance favourably; it had after all spurred conversation in the otherwise reticent Aurelia. In retrospect, it didn't feel like a victory, considering the unnerving way our rendezvous had ended. Now knowing the fate of poor Kalinda only worsened my feelings of dread and agitation.

181

I glanced at the clock and stood. "I guess I should head to class."

"If that is what you wish. I shall hold the fort down here. Aim to be back at the house by three o'clock, earlier if possible. I have an interesting field trip planned for us." Before I could inquire, he stuffed a rather large chunk of boiled egg into his mouth and added while chewing noisily, "This is absolutely scrummy. Are you sure you don't want breakfast?" He offered his bitten toast.

"I want nothing with your saliva on it," I grumbled. "Tell Roksanda I said bye."

As his mouth was too full, I didn't receive a farewell, although that hadn't stopped him from talking before. I left through the patio door and retraced my steps to the front of the house. No one had bothered to lock the door, so I slipped in, returned to our room, and changed into something more suitable for the weather. After collecting my things, I made my escape. It did indeed feel like an escape; yet I couldn't help but watch the house from the bus stop.

Lit by the morning sun, the Richardsons' home looked even more majestic against its bright autumnal backdrop than it had yesterday. Its antiquity, the beautiful façade, the warm-coloured brickwork—all of it pulled me back. But there was something terrible about this beauty, and that urged me to get far away and never return. Unfortunately, I could make no such promise since I was due back in a few hours. But the sight of the approaching bus brought me relief, and as it drew me away to Baker House, the dire happenings that had overwhelmed both my mind and body drifted into the peripheries of my thoughts.

The next couple of hours passed by blissfully. I managed to focus on Professor Farga's lecture on dystopias, utopias, and the apocalypse; they were not exactly heart-warming subjects, but my mind was kept preoccupied. By the time class finished, my appetite returned, and I settled down in a café on campus. It was only when I took a sip of coffee after finishing my sandwich that I thought of Holmes. Where was he right now? What was he doing? He had probably busied himself with a lead or two. In fact, by this time, it was likely that he had made a grand discovery. He may have even captured the true culprit. These thoughts did little to improve my mood. I was already frazzled about finishing William Gibson's *Neuromancer* by next class (being a terribly slow reader, there was no way I could read 271 pages by the following week).

It was nearly three o'clock by the time I found myself on the winding street that led to the Richardsons' home. To my surprise, Holmes and Mr. Richardson were standing outside the front door, engaged in conversation.

"Watson! Excellent timing! We are to accompany Mr. Richardson to the police station," my friend announced when I reached them.

Poor Mr. Richardson looked so distraught that he either didn't notice my arrival or didn't have the energy to acknowledge it. He walked past me wordlessly and climbed into the glistening, black car that was now parked in front of the open garage. Holmes followed suit, but only after muttering, "The Bentley Continental GT" in admiration, and for my benefit since I knew nothing about cars. The reader will be spared details on how I nearly drooled over the dark leather interior of the car. In my defence, I don't often sit in the lap of luxury. I will also skip descriptions of the police station, and my feelings on being inside one for the first time in my life. It is sufficient to say that the experience was somewhat intimidating but thrilling as well. If Holmes were to ever read this account, he would say such frivolous details are a waste of time and would not rest until I had crossed out the entire section. So, without pedantic delay, I proceed to our meeting with Aurelia Richardson.

We waited for nearly an hour before we saw her. I had had the foresight to bring *Necromancer* with me and spent the time reading while Holmes twiddled his thumb restlessly. We were only permitted a fifteen-minute interview while Mr. Richardson spoke to the family lawyer. Holmes seemed satisfied with this, but I was vastly disappointed. What could we learn in so short a time?

The room we found ourselves in after our long wait was small, cold, and had no windows. The walls were a bleak grey, and there was a table at the centre with chairs placed on either side. A stony-faced officer stood by the door— for our protection, we were told. He stared straight ahead and didn't acknowledge us as we took our seats. I looked forward to seeing his face soften with bemusement once Sherlock Holmes opened his mouth.

Aurelia was already there when we arrived. She was still wearing her nightgown, but someone had had the courtesy to offer her a thick cardigan. She looked as comfortable as anyone would be with one wrist handcuffed to the bar that had been installed on the table. What was pitiful was her meek frame and the dark circles around her eyes. Did she recognize us? Was she even aware of what was happening to her? Judging by her vacant expression, I guessed no. However, I was in for a surprise.

"Good afternoon, Dr. Richardson," Holmes greeted, and I offered a small smile. The smile was not returned, but the woman gave us a solemn nod.

"Sherlock Holmes and Janah Watson," she said. She spoke slowly, but there was clarity in her speech. Contrary to my quick assumption, she appeared to be fully aware of everything. "I'm surprised to see you here."

185

"And I am surprised to see you in handcuffs," Holmes responded. "The day has been full of surprises. Awful surprises, if I may add."

Aurelia shrugged. "It's what they do to murderers. I've been in them before."

"But you shouldn't be in them now since you did *not* hurt Mrs. H."

I couldn't quite decipher Aurelia's expression. There was perhaps a hint of astonishment, but something more shone through—a fierce determination of sorts.

"I stabbed Martha, just like I stabbed Ruth and—" Her voice broke.

"Do you remember stabbing your colleague and graduate students?"

"Yes, I do."

"And do you remember stabbing Mrs. H?"

"I—uh—"

Holmes smiled grimly. "Just as I thought. You are assuming you did the deed because of what happened in your past and because the knife was in your hands. Believe me when I say that you did *not* hurt Mrs. H. I intend to prove this. Right now, I expect your full cooperation in obliging me, even though the topic of our discussion will be immensely upsetting for you."

I gulped. I had a strong suspicion that I wasn't going to like the direction this conversation was about to take. Aurelia didn't look very happy either, and it turned out she had good reason.

"I need to know more about the Place," Holmes declared.

His words demonstrated exactly how much fear can be bottled up in a person. Aurelia's features contorted, her eyes bulged, and her lips parted—her face became the very picture of mortification. In a strained voice, she said, "How did you know about it?"

"I've always been good at finding information," Holmes replied. "Also, you have mentioned it yourself. Now, if you will oblige me, please tell me what the Place looks like."

The poor woman's lips trembled, and I braced myself, ready to hear a torrent of cries. But somehow Aurelia mastered herself. Although the voice that emerged was shaky, she spoke coherently.

"It's a terrible place, a place in the forest that shows you how you're going to die."

I couldn't help but shudder along with her. Holmes remained statuesque, of course, but his eyes glittered as though something exciting was unfolding.

"And did it show you how you were going to die?" I asked nervously.

"Of course, it did. Dr. Richardson has already told us this," Holmes interrupted.

Even before Aurelia's whispered response, I remember the words she had uttered the first time we had set foot in her house, made all the more vivid by the thick rope that had been knotted around her neck—death by hanging.

Holmes didn't seem bothered by this recollection, for he sounded rather jolly when he said to Aurelia, "Ah, luckily for you, the last hanging occurred in the 1960s, and capital punishment in that form or any other form is no longer used in this country. Unless, you do the deed yourself, of course, which I strongly discourage you from doing since that does not prove the Place was correct."

"Holmes!" I said, raising my voice.

"What? I didn't do—anyway, if you can continue with your description of the Place, Dr. Richardson?"

"There are trees everywhere," Aurelia responded instantly, "but they grow so tall they block out all light. There are no animals or birds; there is no sound. Eventually, you lose sight and the rest of your senses. And then—and then, a vision of death—"

Holmes considered this for a moment and then pulled out his cell phone, tapped the screen a few times, and showed Aurelia something. I craned my neck to see. Although I could tell that the screen displayed an image, the details were obscured by my angle.

"Is this what it looks like?" he asked.

Aurelia looked taken aback, but she managed to nod. "You took a picture of it."

"Quite so. Is there anything different about it?"

Aurelia took another look, then nodded hesitantly.

Holmes looked quite satisfied as he put the phone away and I slumped into my seat, disappointed. "Don't get comfortable, Watson. We are leaving." To Aurelia, he said, "You won't be in here for too long. I promise you that."

As we stood, I noticed that the policeman was wearing a very peculiar expression. He stared at Holmes as though he were a curio. It was not an unfamiliar sight.

Chapter 12 Art and Artifice

He was, I take it, the most perfect reasoning and observing machine that the world has seen, but as a lover he would have placed himself in a false position.

—Sir Arthur Conan Doyle, *A Scandal in Bohemia*

WE EXITED THE POLICE STATION FIVE MINUTES later. Mr. Richardson had stayed behind, so we were left to wander home by ourselves. The autumn chill, and perhaps the aftereffects of our interview with Aurelia, made me shudder as we began our walk to the subway, which thankfully was only a block away. The aroma of coffee drifted in the air as we passed a café. Despite my resolution to stay caffeine-free in the evenings, I was very tempted to go in. However, there was an urgency to Holmes' steps that permitted no detour. He had consulted his watch as we had left the interrogation room, and I could tell that he was unhappy with how much time we had spent at the police station. I didn't know if we were going back to campus or the Richardsons' home, but I felt reluctant to ask, knowing that the response would be snappy, vague, or a combination of both. There was also the possibility that I had misjudged the situation; Holmes may have been in as much of a hurry as I was to get indoors and leave behind the cold.

But Holmes was acting peculiar in another way as well. There was a grim satisfaction on his face that I couldn't explain. If I didn't know any better, I would say he had solved the case. Yet what had we accomplished by our visit to the police station? Holmes had succeeded in invoking terror, albeit a temporary one, in a woman who would likely face a grim future. He had also gotten a description of the Place, but how that related to Mrs. Hudson's attack, I hadn't the slightest clue. I also didn't know how it could help free Aurelia. Adding to the mystery was the photo of the Place on Holmes' phone. How had he photographed something rumoured to exist on some far-off island? And when had he had the opportunity to do this?

Although I was teeming with questions, finding out how Holmes had spent the morning took precedence. I didn't expect a detailed answer, but when a red light halted our speed walking, I cleared my throat loudly and said, "So what did you do this morning after I left? You didn't sit around flirting with Roksanda, did you?" The latter remark, the answer to which I knew would be a definite "no", had been cunningly added in the hopes of instigating an immediate and heated reply. It worked as planned.

"To quote someone from your own area of interest," Holmes began indignantly, "'I am not a man to be moved by a pretty face. There is a grinning skull beneath it, and men like me who look and work below the surface see that, and not its delicate covering.'"

I blinked like an idiot. The quote seemed somewhat familiar —

"*Nicholas Nickleby* by Charles Dickens." After a lofty glare, he continued, "Since you finished the book only in late August, I wrongly assumed that passages from the story would be fresh in your memory."

Although I hadn't meant to, I gasped loudly. The book in question lay buried in a drawer in my room, and I had never mentioned it to Holmes; there was simply no way he could have known what I had read over the summer.

"How did you know that? Tell me!" The command was disembogued loudly enough to attract the attention of passersby, who looked at me nervously and retreated in haste. Holmes, on the other hand, remained unfazed. In fact, he glared at me for a moment longer before his expression softened. This may have been due to the steadfast way I held his gaze, or perhaps the comic sight of my pink ears and runny nose had eased him. Whatever the reason—I preferred to think it was the former—he proceeded to answer my question without making me beg first.

"One day, while you were out attending classes, I took the liberty of entering your room to look for a magnifying glass. I had misplaced mine and was in desperate need of one. No, Watson, you did not leave your room unlocked by accident—I simply picked the lock. It was while I was going through your drawers that I came across *Nicholas Nickleby*. I immediately knew it was not a library book; you would not have stowed it away deep in drawer if it had been. It looked rather withered, obviously purchased second hand, very possibly from the used book sale the local library runs every month. This I confirmed by the library stamp on the first page and the receipt left in one of the pages.

"While you were at the library that day, you also picked up the special edition bookmark that was being given away to celebrate its 100th anniversary—during the first week of August, if memory serves me correctly. You see, I had arrived a few weeks before the start of school to familiarize myself with the city, and had received a bookmark myself. One can never have too many bookmarks!" Without pausing for breath, he went on, "Anyway, that key detail allowed me to deduce when you had started the book. Based on the page count and my knowledge of your reading speed, which is dismally low by the way, I estimate you finished it by the end of August."

The logic was sound as always, and I would have been thoroughly satisfied with the explanation if I hadn't known that he had rummaged through my things. Oddly enough, I was less bothered and more intrigued by this — the admission and the simple way he had expressed it showcased his eccentricity to a grand, new level. What was equally astounding was the idea of Holmes perusing a work of fiction, but I didn't bother verifying if he had actually read the book or picked up the quote by chance. I had, after all, stumbled upon a third, and rather juicier, discovery.

"So you think Roksanda is pretty, eh," I smirked. The signs had been apparent from the start — he had watched her like a hawk on more than one occasion, not to mention how smoothly he had linked arms with her that very morning. Holmes naturally admitted nothing. In fact, his severe grimace would have convinced anyone else that he was not engrossed by a petite blonde with honey eyes. Wisely deciding that it was time to steer the conversation back to its initial purpose, I asked again what he had done that morning.

"Well," Holmes began, "eating a heavy meal was a mistake. I just couldn't think! Next time, I think it will be wise to abstain from food so that digestion doesn't interfere. I managed to clear by head by taking a long stroll into the city core and ended up at the art gallery. I felt inclined to go in, partly because I have never been before, and it proved to be a good distraction. What are your thoughts on the revitalization of the building, by the way? I hear there was some criticism." Without waiting for an answer, he went on eagerly, possibly relieved that we were no longer talking about how pretty Roksanda was. "I must admit that the glass and wood façade is one of Gehry's more inconspicuous designs, but I rather enj—"

"What were you doing at the art gallery?" I had to interrupt. When done intermittently, listening to Holmes' banter on his various subjects of interest was a somewhat entertaining pastime. However, he was a didactic speaker capable of spewing endless volumes of speech. Hence, a rude interruption was necessary to ensure I received the answer I was waiting for.

"That is a silly question, Watson. People go to art galleries to see art, which is what I did. The gallery has an impressive collection from Canadian artists. You have lived here for more than a year now so I assume you have already seen the permanent collections? Anyway, there is a fascinating exhibition on right now that documents the impact of humans on the planet. Did you know that the artists went to nearly every continent to compile this data? It was quite revelatory — Drat! We've missed the light!"

195

He frowned and shot me an accusatory look as though I were to blame. His frown deepened after another glance at his watch. "No, this won't do. We need to get back to the house right away. Where is a taxi when you need one?! Keep up, Watson!"

Puzzled though I was, I ran after a frantic Holmes, smiling smugly at the realization that he had said *city*. Twice.

*

It turned out "house" referred to the Richardsons' place, and we may have arrived sooner by subway. Despite his enormous brain, Holmes hadn't predicted how disruptive rush hour traffic could be. As a result, we had sat idle in our cab for quite some time. I had watched the innumerable masses of travellers around us while Holmes had twiddled his fingers impatiently and muttered insults.

By the time we arrived about forty minutes later, Holmes' impatience had reached its zenith. He practically jumped out of the vehicle and rushed into the house, leaving me to handle the fare. I didn't understand his haste, and since he had not offered an explanation and thwarted my attempts at conversation during the ride, my own mood was anything but cheerful. Grumpily, I paid the cab driver and rushed towards the house, propelled by both the chill and curiosity. The front door was unlocked; Mr. Richardson had not locked it on his way out, and neither Roksanda nor Aurora had bothered to lock up after him. This was hardly comforting; I now wondered if the door had been left unlocked last night. I certainly didn't remember anyone locking the patio door after we had returned to the house yesterday. The thought sent a chill up my spine—how vulnerable we would have been in our beds!

Upon entering, the first thing I noticed was that Holmes had disappeared. I crept up to *the* hallway, careful to avert my eyes, although I could see the drying blood and Mrs. Hudson's slippers in my peripherals. There appeared to be no movement in the kitchen, so I backed away and headed to the room we had spent the night. It had been tidied up, and the only sign of Holmes was his backpack, which sat on the reclining chair. I then loitered by the stairs for a moment and contemplated ascending to Aurelia's room. I was about to make the climb when faint voices reached me. My ears perked, and I stepped into the hallway that led to the library, following the muffled sound of someone talking.

Just as I had predicted, Holmes was standing in the massive doorway of the library. Sensing my presence, or more likely hearing my footsteps thudding along the hallway, he moved aside jerkily to let me in. It was quite apparent his temper hadn't waned. My nose suddenly crinkled.

"What's that sm—" I stopped, noticing Roksanda by the fireplace. She was hovering over the flames, rubbing her hands furiously. When she saw me, she straightened and waved. I returned the wave but lingered by Holmes for just a moment.

"What's wrong? Did she refuse to give you her number?" I whispered, smirking.

Holmes' gaze narrowed. In barely audible tones, he said, "As a matter of fact, I've already gotten her number."

I joined Roksanda by the fire, pondering this response as my face and fingertips soaked in the warmth. Holmes followed sullenly and sat down on the loveseat, keeping his slender figure unnaturally stiff. One long leg hung over the other, and his fingers clasped one another. He stared at the fire with the same intensity I had seen that morning. Roksanda threw me a questioning glance, and I shrugged and repeated my question.

"What is that smell? It smells like—"

"Burning hair," Holmes interrupted rather loudly. "Or perhaps feathers?"

Roksanda shrugged. "The room smelled fine when I got here. It was only when I got the fire going did the smell come. Maybe something fell in the fireplace?"

"Indeed," came the jeering response.

I sighed. "Holmes, is something bothering you?"

"Obviously! Is that not apparent? I am, in fact, very bothered right now, Watson. I am bothered by the fact that I am an idiot. If it should ever

198

strike you that I am getting a little overconfident in my abilities, kindly remind me of this precise moment."

Again, the housekeeper and I exchanged bemused looks. Holmes undoubtedly perceived our confusion, but it only made him grumble incoherently. Deciding it was best to let him self-soothe for a moment, I turned my attention to Roksanda.

"We went to see Aurelia," I said.

"I figured that's where you went. I saw you both get into the car with Mr. Richardson. Poor man. He looked devastated. I didn't even have a chance to talk to him. He dropped off his luggage, grabbed his car keys, and practically ran out the door again. Your friend managed to grab his attention though."

"Yeah, he's pretty good at doing that." I glanced at Holmes, who took no notice of our conversation. His brows were furrowed, and his hooded eyes were half closed.

"How is Aurelia doing?" Roksanda asked. "She must be terrified being there all alone. They won't charge her, right? They can't do that to her. She's sick and needs help. Mr. Richardson can't deny that any —"

That was when a thought occurred to me. "Where's Mrs. Richardson?"

"Who knows where that old hag is," glowered a bitter voice.

With the exception of Holmes, who remained meditatively still, Roksanda and I turned to find

Aurora standing in the doorway, holding a small bowl and spoon. I wondered how long she had lingered there, listening to our conversation. She eyed us for a moment, then slurped the soupy contents of her spoon loudly. Now that her presence had been announced, she thrust her protruding belly forward, marched in, and slumped down next to Holmes, which caused splotches of soup to splash across her white blouse. Holmes looked annoyed at first, possibly due to her pervasive perfume or because she hadn't chosen one of the other empty seats. Thankfully, he kept any rude remarks to himself and soon shifted his focus to Aurora's blouse. It apparently warranted the same intense scrutiny he had given her belly the day before, although I had no idea why.

"What's that supposed to mean?" I asked. "Are you saying you don't know where she is?"

The response didn't come right away since Aurora, having noticed the soup stains, scowled and began rubbing them. That only worsened the damage, however, much to her chagrin. Roksanda snickered quietly next to me, which luckily went unnoticed by Aurora. Sighing, she gave up and said, "Maybe she's in Milan or maybe she's somewhere here. Either way, she's probably maxing out dad's credit cards as we speak."

"That is a rather vague response," Holmes said snippily.

Aurora huffed, "Dad and Portia were at the airport when she suddenly said she felt sick. She told him to go on, saying she'd meet him in Milan, and checked into the airport hotel. Dad hasn't had news of her since."

"Has Mr. Richardson tried calling her? Perhaps to explain what has happened at home?" Holmes asked. "No? Has he at least sent a text? Another no. Hm, and she hasn't done anything to contact him either? How sinister."

"Do you think something's happened to her?" Roksanda asked. Perhaps I had imagined it, but she looked rather hopeful.

"Oh, I am sure she is fine," Holmes replied airily. To Aurora, he added, "But your father and stepmother are in desperate need of marriage counselling."

Roksanda snorted and then covered her mouth apologetically, and Aurora rolled her eyes. I, on the other hand, was thinking about Mrs. Richardson's disappearance. Holmes seemed convinced that nothing horrible had happened to her; was that because he knew more than he let on? I wondered if he had considered the possibility that had crept into my head.

"Well, I hope you're right about Mrs. Richardson being okay," Roksanda said. Again, her tone wasn't very convincing. Perhaps she had realized what a terrible liar she was since she added very quickly, "Ah, look at the time! I think I'll head home now. I'd better put out the fire—unless you three plan to stay?"

Our discomfort in one another's presence was apparent in how rigorously we shook our heads.

"Watson and I will be leaving now," Holmes said. "We have plenty of homework to catch up on, having done very little this weekend." He looked rather happy at the prospect of doing homework. "Poor Watson is quite stressed that she has to finish *Necromancer* in a matter of days, although it really should take no longer than two days, but she is a rather slow reader—"

A nasty glance from me encouraged him to stop talking and stand up to button his coat. His deduction didn't impress me very much; he had seen me with the book at the police station and knew I often complained that my professors never gave us enough time to read—and enjoy—course material. What surprised me was the sudden change in his mood. Holmes had entered the room sour-tempered, but now he was almost jubilant. What had happened in the last few minutes to alter his mood? I suspected something other than chemistry problems and readings had lifted his spirits.

Aurora stood as well, mumbled a farewell, and exited the room without waiting for our goodbyes. I didn't care much; every conversation I had had with the woman only magnified my unfavourable opinion of her. My mind was preoccupied with more important things like returning to Baker House and curling up in the library with a fresh picking from one of the dusty shelves. Unfortunately, I was not to experience this bliss for some hours to come.

Roksanda took the spray bottle from the mantle and began putting out the fire. The smell of smoke wafted into my nose as she poked the firewood and embers with a fire poker and continued spraying. I glanced at Holmes; he was staring at the damp wood as though hypnotized.

"May I?" he asked, extending a hand.

He took the poker from Roksanda and began sifting through the dark ash. When he straightened a moment later and put the poker back in the black steel stand that housed all the fireplace tools, he looked grim again. His lips, the margins of which had been rolled in to reveal a very thin line in the place of his mouth, imparted nothing though. He tucked his hands inside his pockets and looked ready to leave.

"I'm going to go get my things," Roksanda began. "Want to meet in the foyer? We can all head out to—" She was interrupted by the ringing of Holmes' phone, which he pulled out of his coat pocket and answered. The call lasted only one minute, during which time Holmes looked as impassive as ever, then mumbled a response, and hung up.

"Was that about Mrs. Hudson?" I asked. "Is she going to be okay?"

Holmes' eyes sparkled. "That was Mr. Richardson. He just got a call from the hospital, saying that Mrs. H will be making a full recovery. She is out of the ICU and is awake now. He is on his way here to pick us up so that we can go see her. Homework will have to wait, Watson. Will you join us, Roksanda?"

"I will, but first I need to go home to feed my cat. I'll meet you both at the hospital." To Holmes, she added, "You can text me the details."

So he had been telling the truth about the phone number after all. Regardless, I was still surprised, for Sherlock Holmes didn't strike me as the type who would do such a thing. I could hardly describe him as romantic, or even mildly poetic, but perhaps I didn't know him well enough to make such an assessment. Tempted though I was to tease him again once Roksanda had left, I steered the conversation back to the case.

"Do you think Mrs. Hudson will remember anything?" I asked. "If she does, she'll be able to confirm my suspicion."

Holmes raised an eyebrow. "And what may that be?"

I hesitated. On a handful of occasions, I have made the mistake of sharing thoughts—and sometimes theories—with Holmes. If the topic was one he was well-versed in, he took pride in ridiculing my ideas and unceremoniously broadcasting their flaws. Unfortunately for me, his brain teemed with a plethora of knowledge on the dreadful subject of crime; I could recall at least half a dozen times when a crime statistic had been incidentally introduced into a discussion. Hence, I braced myself for a belittling rebuttal before speaking.

"I think Mrs. Richardson may have been the one who attacked Mrs. Hudson. No one can account for her whereabouts last night."

Holmes remained as unmoved as ever as he asked, "And what would motivate her to do such a thing?"

"It's simple. She's embarrassed by Aurelia and wants her out of the house, which is why she attacked Mrs. Hudson and made it look like Aurelia did it. That way she gets institutionalized again."

"That is a most compelling theory. Good work, Watson," he said, then smirked. "I like this theory far more than the previous one of diabolical forces interfering with the affairs of men."

"And women," I added.

"Of course. Women as well, especially since women are central to this problem. Both victims and perpetrator are female after all."

"Does that mean you agree with me?" I grew excited as all sorts of wild ideas took root. "Maybe we should tell the police, or we can go straight to the hotel and search—"

"I am sure the police are already wasting their time with this line of inquiry. I've no doubt Mr. Richardson has suggested this to them. The poor man is understandably desperate to save his daughter."

Despite trying, it was difficult to keep my disappointment at bay. "Wasting their time? So you don't think Mrs. Richardson had anything to do with what happened?"

Holmes chuckled and looked at me as though I were a child in need of a slow, simple-worded explanation. "I am saying," he drawled, "that I knew the identity of the culprit before Mrs. H's attack." I stared at him incredulously, but before I could question him further, he continued, "I haven't any proof, unfortunately, which is the task I will be occupied with for the next hour or so. I really can't say how long it will take. In the meantime, I need you to stay here. I will call you with further instructions."

"But isn't Mr. Richardson picking us up?"

"What? Oh. I lied about that."

Sensing my impending questions and protestations, he spun around with extraordinary speed and headed for the door. I had to practically leap to grab his coat sleeve.

"Wait! Did you know Mrs. Hudson was going to be attacked?"

"I am *not* clairvoyant, Watson."

"Then how did you know in advance that she would be attacked?"

"Ah, but I said no such thing." Holmes smiled ominously. "I said I knew who the culprit was, the person behind what we were initially called in to investigate."

"Aurelia's haunting."

"Ugh, that appellation makes me cringe, but yes, that is what I was referring to, and before you ask, there is indeed a connection between that and Mrs. H's attack. Time is of the essence, Watson, so I must be off." He yanked his arm free and left the library, his long coat swishing behind him. And then, all was silent.

I waited for a little over five minutes, consumed with anger and irritation the whole time, before exiting the room. Holmes' promise of "further instructions" had been said in the same way a parent would task something "important" to a child. He simply wanted me out of his way, but I refused to sit idly while he carried out clandestine missions.

As I tiptoed out of the library and down the hallway, my paranoia that Holmes was hiding somewhere, ready to reprimand me for not following orders, vanished. My mind was now occupied by another distraction, for as I reached the foyer, hushed voices sounded. I pulled back, pressing my body flat along the wall. But unable to resist my curiosity, I snuck a quick peek a moment later.

A man and woman were standing at the foot of the stairs, locked in embrace. I immediately recognized Aurora's red hair, but the man was a stranger. He was tall, well-built, and dressed neatly in a thick cardigan, collared shirt, and jeans. His longish dark hair had been combed back to reveal a pale, bearded face that looked worn even though he couldn't have been much older than Aurora. I didn't need to be Sherlock Holmes to detect a passionate intimacy between the pair.

Finally ending the kiss, the man mumbled something. I quickly pulled back as his eyes wandered nervously around the foyer.

Aurora's reply rang clearly, "Dad won't be home for another couple of hours, but I guess we'll be safer in my room."

The man responded in low, inaudible tones, but he seemed to agree with her. He still looked anxious as they went down the hallway to Aurora's bedroom, oblivious of my presence. It was just as they disappeared from view that I noticed the silver wedding band on the man's ring finger. Was he Aurora's husband or was she seeing a married man? The former didn't seem likely considering what Roksanda had told us, which left the latter as the only logical option. I didn't think too much about this, however. It was no business of mine unless, of course, Aurora's lover was somehow connected to our investigation...

I waited until I heard the door shut and then resumed my burglar-like creeping. It was only when I had exited the house and sprinted down the lawn past the open gate and onto the street that I took a deep, refreshing breath. The bitterly cold air froze my lungs instantly, and I contemplated returning to the warmth of the Richardson house — for only a moment. The thought of Holmes sleuthing without me forbade such an action.

An intimidating darkness was beginning to settle on the surrounding jungle of opulent homes. The empty street, unfortunately, held no trace of Holmes. After a hefty shiver, I headed southwest since the opposite direction only went deeper into the neighbourhood, and I saw no reason for Holmes to go that way. Praying that my deduction was correct, I assumed a speedy trot.

Fifteen minutes later, I reached the end of the road and turned onto the bridge that would lead me back to the comforting sight of crowded, bustling streets. Up ahead I could finally see Holmes meandering behind a few other pedestrians. I imagined him spinning around to apprehend me after hearing my footsteps, although this would have been impossible at such a distance, regardless of how well one's ears worked. But a paranoid brain rarely yields to logic.

My solitary walk lasted mere minutes. As I left the bridge and crossed the bustling intersection, a torrent of people rushed out of a nearby bus and shuffled into the adjacent subway entrance *en masse*. I didn't dare break the continuous stream of commuters for fear of being shoved or swept underground with them. By the time they passed, however, Holmes was nowhere to be seen.

Bemused, I squinted, hoping to spot the grey of his coat, but since the rest of the city seemed to be coloured in similar shades, it was a pointless task. Perhaps that was why the flash of red in the distance caught my attention. My flicker of recognition never reached fruition though because at that exact moment—

"Watson!" cried a belligerent voice.

Chapter 13 Captured

...I seemed to see something terrible – a creature of infinite patience and craft, with a smiling face and a murderous heart.

—Sir Arthur Conan Doyle, *The Hound of the Baskervilles*

IGNORING AN IRATE PERSON SELDOM PACIFIES A situation. For that reason, I turned slowly, the heat already rising in my cheeks, to face a scowling, wool-clad Holmes. My apprehension, however, dissolved at the sight of his ears, which had turned bright pink in the cold, giving him a comical, elvish appearance.

"Oh, hi, Holmes. Fancy seeing you here," I chirped.

He grunted at my attempt to imitate his mannerism, but his voice had softened when he responded, "I told you to stay put. What are you doing here? You could have at least brought my

211

rucksack. Now I have to return to the Richardsons' house to fetch it."

I ignored the last bit. "I have something important to tell you that may be related to the case."

"You can tell me as we walk."

"A man came to the house after you left," I said, once we began walking again. "He and Aurora were kissing."

"Oh? How interesting." But Holmes didn't sound very impressed. "A tall bloke, athletic, black hair, beard, and attached earlobes—does that match his description?"

I stared at him, astonished. "Uh, yes. Not sure about the earlobes though."

"Pity no one pays attention to the human ear. The ridges and furrows of the outer ear are quite useful for identification. There is an excellent paper on the morphological variations of the ear that I will email you once we are back at Baker House."

I had no intention of reading the "excellent" paper in question but made no objection—an offended Holmes was a reticent one, and I was eager to know how he had come to know of Aurora's visitor. Unfortunately, he continued his discussion of ears, now quoting word for word some passages from the paper mentioned above. I gently steered him back to the mysterious man.

"Oh, him. He is her husband."

"How did you know that?"

"I saw their wedding photo in Aurora's bedroom."

"You went into her bedroom?"

"Yes, I believe that is what I just said. Oh, don't look at me as though I am some common criminal. I was trying to solve the second case since I had some time to spare," Holmes insisted, quickening his pace.

"The second case?" I asked, struggling to keep up.

"Will you stop repeating what I say? It is a tiresome habit."

"I didn't realize there was a second case."

"No one else did either. Anyway, more on that later. Right now, we have a more sinister business to take care of." He came to a sudden stop, and grabbing my arm, ducked behind the hedgerow that divided two houses.

Having been consumed by conversation for the last quarter of an hour, I hadn't noticed the startling transition of my surroundings. Gone were the noisy, lively streets; they had been replaced with a quiet road, lined with rather seedy-looking homes. Light flickered in most of them, which helped diminish the darkness that beleaguered us. It didn't ease the sting of the whistling wind though, which felt colder now that we had come to a stop. Unsurprisingly, Holmes wasn't shivering miserably like me. His slender form had a statuesque steadiness to it as his gaze scrutinized something in the distance.

The object of his interest was rather unextraordinary; it was a small, two-storey house that nearly blended in with the night since every light was off. A moment later, the porch lights flickered on, and a figure glided up to the door.

I stared in astonishment. "You're following Roksanda?!"

"Tsk, tsk. I gave you too much credit, Watson. I thought you would have noticed the red coat and familiar gait of the Richardsons' housekeeper by now."

"I did recog—"

"Did you at least realize she was lying about the cat? No? Oh, Watson, there was not a single cat hair upon her person. You should have realized Roksanda has no cat."

"Argh! Just tell me what we're doing here. It's getting really cold."

"There is no use in complaining. I did, after all, ask you to remain at the house. I am rather surprised you choose to follow me instead of reading by the fire." There was a twinkle in his eyes as he said this, and I wondered if he actually approved my disobedience.

"Well, to be frank with you," I began, "I have no idea how to light a fire in a fireplace. I grew up in an apartment, Holmes." This confession elicited a chuckle. "Anyway, how could I have helped with the case by staying put?"

"Your job was to call Roksanda as soon as I gave you the signal via text and create an emergency to draw her out of her rooms. You would then keep her detained while I searched her place."

"Oh." So I had an actual role to play in the finale after all! I had little time to feel appeased about the inclusion or apologetic for wrecking the meticulously laid-out plan though; the gravity of Holmes' scheme struck me. "Hold on, are you saying you were going to break into her home? But that would be breaking the law!" I exclaimed.

"Ah, you appear to be opposed to breaking the law. Shame!" Holmes smiled roguishly. "I assume that means you would do nothing that risks arrest? No? Pooh! What if it was for a worthy cause? Such as proving Dr. Richardson's innocence."

I hesitated. "Well—"

Holmes' smile widened, the mischief replaced by something warm and genuine. "I knew I could rely on you. Don't worry, there will be no breaking required. You see, I have the keys." He patted his coat pocket. "I took them earlier from her purse. I do hope the owner has spare keys hidden somewhere on the property. Ah, fret not, Watson," he added, misinterpreting my look of alarm. "You have not completely sabotaged my plans. I have changed them anyhow. All we have to do is wait." There was an excited quiver to his voice.

I turned my attention back to the figure on the porch, having missed the part where it had frantically fumbled around for the keys. Roksanda was now bending over some flowerpots that sat on the porch. She straightened a moment later, having found what we assumed were the spare keys. As soon as she had disappeared inside the house, Holmes rubbed his palms energetically.

"We will give her ten minutes," he murmured.

Not knowing what Holmes expected to happen, I fidgeted with anticipation, forgetting the cold for a moment, and stared at the porch, ready to act with little notice. Inside some lights flickered on. Two minutes passed and the porch lights shut off, but my eyes continued to dart anxiously. After waiting for nearly fifteen minutes in silence, however, I turned to Holmes doubtingly. He himself looked perturbed.

"I suppose we will have to draw her out after all and then conduct our search," he said grumpily. "It shouldn't take long to search a single room though, and I know exactly what to look for." He added, for my benefit, "No, Watson, she is not the owner of this house. She can hardly afford to take the bus in so drab a weather. She is renting a room in this house."

"I can still make the call," I offered.

Holmes frowned, scanning the vicinity, and muttered something that sounded quite like "this blasted wind". Sighing, he pressed his phone into my palm. "Yes, make the call."

"Somehow you managed to steal her keys and get her number," I muttered, scrolling through his contacts. "Here I thought your brain governed your heart."

"It does," he said triumphantly. "Stealing the keys was far easier than getting the number since only stealthy hands were required for the first. Convincing acting was needed for the second. Luckily, I am adept at both. You see, I had to feign interest in her to get the number."

I nearly laughed out loud. "I can't believe you managed to flirt with a girl." But seeing the scowl that was beginning to form on his face, I quickly said, "What emergency should I make up? Er, how about I say Aurora went into labour early?"

To my surprise, Holmes shook his head vigorously. "Certainly not. Anything but that will draw Roksanda out of the house."

"Oh, come on. She can't hate Aurora that much. I'm sure she'll come."

"It has nothing to do with hatred, Watson. Just tell her the bathroom has flooded, and Mr. Richardson wants her to take care of it."

I made the call. Although I didn't possess my friend's aptitude for theatrics, I did a fair job of conveying the problem in the most frantic voice I could muster and hung up a moment later, having confirmation that Roksanda would arrive at the house shortly.

We waited for a few minutes and then scrambled to crouch low as she emerged from

217

the house. Thankfully, the blackness of the night kept our presence veiled, and the housekeeper strode by us, none the wiser. We watched as she walked to the end of the street and came to a stop at the bus shelter. About ten minutes later, the bus arrived, picked up its lone passenger, and disappeared, and we were finally able to leave our hiding place.

"Come, Watson, the game is afoot!" Holmes cried and bounded towards the house.

The presence of the (stolen) key did nothing to shrink my uneasiness; I had never broken into anyone's home before and I had a despairing feeling that it would not be the last time if I were to continue my friendship with Sherlock Holmes. A thrilling excitement soon made my body throb and overtook my panic as we entered Roksanda's home with stealth and speed. Prepared as always, Holmes had the good sense to bring white rubber gloves, which I gratefully pulled over my pink, frozen fingers just before we went inside.

The house was as unremarkable on the inside as it was on the outside. From what I could make out in the dark—Roksanda had turned off the lights on her way out—there was a sparsely furnished living room, an extremely narrow hallway that led to the back of the house, and an equally cramped staircase that led upstairs. Pulling out his flashlight, Holmes proceeded immediately to the second floor and began systematically checking all the bedrooms, revealing dark, empty rooms or closets. His head drew back suddenly from one of these rooms, causing me to bump into him. He quietly closed the door, then whirled around, finger at his lips.

"One of Roksanda's roommates is sound asleep in there. We'd best be as silent as possible," he whispered, glancing at his watch. "Not even half past seven yet. The people are so peculiar here." He failed to comment on his own irregular sleeping habits, which sometimes consisted of no sleep at all. I was fairly certain I hadn't dreamt every instance of marching footsteps from the room next door.

I grunted in response, then followed as Holmes peaked inside the next room, the door to which was ajar. He switched on the lights.

"This is the one," he announced.

The small room we had stepped into was littered with a dizzying excess of belongings. Holmes, accustomed to the slovenly clutter of his Baker House room, meandered through the space gracefully. I followed, tripping only once over a backpack that lay on the floor.

"What are we looking for?" I asked, scanning the bed, dresser, desk, and wooden easel that stood by the window. With interest, I peered at the canvas that sat on it. The housekeeper was working on an Arctic landscape in her spare time, and it was coming along nicely. I wagered this was the clue Holmes had used to identify the correct room.

Ignoring my question, Holmes said, "Let's see how good your memory is. What was Roksanda wearing yesterday?"

"Um, a brown sweater, grey jogging pants, and really thick socks."

Holmes seemed both satisfied and irritated by my response. "Excellent, Watson. Quite unfortunate about those socks. Now, did her sweater have pockets?"

I had no idea what was so unfortunate about the socks, apart from the fact that aesthetically they looked dreadful. I remained silent on this point though and tried to picture the housekeeper's sweater instead. This turned out to be a waste of time and brain cells since Holmes answered his own question with gusto.

"There were no pockets! Which only leaves the pants. That is the first thing we are searching for—grey jogging pants. Ask no questions now, Watson. I will explain everything in due time." There was lustre in his eyes, and his whole body seemed to quiver with anticipation. The mood was contagious.

We began our search, Holmes starting with the closet while I inspected the clothes that lay on the chair by the desk. Despite keeping the Richardson house spotless, it turned out Roksanda was as neat as Holmes when it came to putting her clothes away. I soon found the pants buried in the heap and waved it in the air. Holmes rushed over, grabbed it with one gloved hand, and began turning out the pockets with the other. I watched, feeling anxious, despite having little idea of what was transpiring.

"Ha!" he cried. "Here is our evidence."

"Is that—" I began.

"Blood!" He handed the pants back to me, and I held the "evidence" at arm's length, staring distastefully at the small, dried bloodstain that blotched one of the exposed pockets. Was that Mrs. Hudson's blood? No opportunity to voice this suspicion was granted, however, since Holmes had sprinted back towards the closet. He emerged victoriously a moment later, holding what looked like a rolled-up poster. This he immediately and very carefully spread open on the bed.

A familiar painting lay before us—a bleak, near-winter landscape with no sun in sight but abounding with barren trees that overlooked a dark lake. It was the same painting that Holmes and I had scrutinized at the Richardsons' home—Aurelia's painting. Yet I was sure I had seen it on the wall that day.

"Are you sure about that, Watson?" my friend asked, examining the work. He then turned it over and scrutinized the blank back. Apparently satisfied with what he had seen, he carried on, "You have been careful to avert your gaze from the hallway. Can you be certain the painting still hangs on the wall?"

"Stop reading my mind," I hissed.

"I read your face. I can outline my chain of reasoning and demonstrate exactly how I arrived at—"

"No, you've done that enough times," I said, scowling. "Just answer one question: is Aurelia's painting missing from the wall?"

"If by that you mean to ask whether there is a gaping emptiness where the frame should be hanging, then no. There is a painting there."

"Then what's this? Why is it here? Is this one a forgery?"

Holmes grinned. "Very good, Watson. It is indeed, but the one in the Richardsons' home is a forgery as well. Ah, you are confused, which is understandable. I have one phone call to make, and then we will leave for Baker House."

He rolled up the painting, placed it back in the closet, and then motioned for me to return the pants to the chair, with the pocket tucked back inside. We then exited the room and left the house, locking the door behind us. The chill had worsened, but that didn't propel Holmes towards Baker House. Instead, he led me to the hedgerow where we had hidden and pulled out his phone. The call he made was to Mr. Richardson.

"Good evening, this is Sherlock Holmes," he said brightly. The tone was ill-suited, but Holmes appeared to not have realized and Mr. Richardson apparently made no remark against it. "Are you still at the police station? Excellent. I have some important information to relay to you about Mrs. H's attack. The culprit is none other than your housekeeper, Roksanda Dragomirov. You will find the evidence to arrest her in her room. I recall you didn't know her home address when I had asked earlier — it is 31 Seaton Lane. If you can instruct the police to look for a pair of grey jogging pants with a bloodied pocket and a painting of a dismal-looking landscape, I will explain everything in person. One car to Roksanda's rooms and another one to the bus stop near your residence, which is probably where she is right now, will suffice. See you soon, Mr. Richardson."

He hung up and turned to me triumphantly. "The final blow has been delivered. We shall remain hidden here until the police come. Roksanda will have surely realized there is no flooded bathroom by now. I expect her to be waiting for the bus, feeling rather confused. She may have even begun to suspect our undertakings here, especially if she heard the wind whistling in the background when you made the call. We can't risk her arriving here before the police and destroying the evidence. She has already done that with the sock. Let's see how persuasive Mr. Richardson can be with the boys in blue."

We didn't wait long. It seemed Mr. Richardson had been quite successful at pushing the authorities into action since a cruiser arrived long before my fingers began to freeze (this actually happened during our walk back to

Baker House, which Holmes insisted on doing rather than taking the bus like a sensible person). We snuck away stealthily once the officers reached the porch.

Neither of us spoke during the walk home. Holmes' excited energy had finally dissipated, but there was a glow to his face and he looked very pleased. I, on the other hand, was one part irritated that no explanation had been offered for all that had happened and two parts tired. The latter was the reason I didn't object to Holmes' reticent adieu as he dropped me off at Baker House and disappeared into the darkness.

I climbed into bed, having only the strength to throw off my jacket and boots, and sleepily wondered what Holmes was doing. That night I dreamt of a lanky young man settling into an armchair with an oversized book on organic chemistry...in the middle of a bustling police station.

Chapter 14 The Conclusion

It was obvious to me that my companion's mind was now made up about the case, although what his conclusions were was more than I could even dimly imagine.

— Sir Arthur Conan Doyle, *The Adventure of the Beryl Coronet*

WHEN I WOKE UP NEARLY TEN HOURS LATER, IT was still dark. Cursing autumn's sunless mornings and frosty weather, I stumbled out of bed stiffly since I was still wearing my jeans and sweater from the day before. It took some effort to pry them off and jump into the shower, but the warmth of the water was worth it. The serenity, however, was short-lived; my thoughts, no longer shielded by sleep-induced oblivion, became woeful as I reflected on the happenings of the last two days. The case had come to a successful finish, and yet there was much I didn't know. Unlike a restless me, the person with the answers was in all probability sleeping soundly next door—although one could never tell what occupied Sherlock Holmes at daybreak. Regardless of what he was doing, I decided to interrupt him since my first class that day wouldn't start for another three hours, and I had nothing better to do.

I did have the courtesy to bring some tea when I marched through his unlocked door after a loud knock. The gesture was greeted with a scowl from Holmes, who sat in his armchair by the open window, smoking a cigarette. The red satin Persian slipper that he used in the place of a cigarette case lay within arm's reach on the bed. Near it sat the simpering skull from the anthropology lab. *Had he spent the entire night smoking?* I wondered. *And talking to the skull.* I thought I had dreamt the muffled voice that sailed through the wall in the wee hours of the morning.

The draft from the window made the room icy cold and spread plumes of smoke everywhere. Holmes, who had wrapped himself in a thick blue bathrobe, appeared unaffected by neither the cold nor the smoke. I, on the other hand, shivered and returned the scowl, which prompted him to reluctantly stub out the cigarette in the ashtray that sat on the windowsill. He then shut the window and turned to me.

"You know I prefer coffee. Some biscuits would have been nice." But he took the mug and sniffed it.

"Well, I couldn't just start grinding coffee beans at six o'clock in the morning," I huffed. "Other people live here in case you haven't noticed. Can't you find a stimulant that doesn't fill the room with smoke?"

"My snuffbox is somewhere here." Grey eyes scanned the room languidly. "You look like you could use a pinch."

"No, thanks," I said irritably.

"Are you sure? Inhalation allows for a quick hit of nicotine—"

"I said no! Wait a minute—why didn't the fire alarm go off?" The atmosphere was certainly poisonous enough to set one off.

Ignoring my astonished look, he answered, "I disabled the one in here. It is a nuisance to go outside every time I want to smoke, so I took care of the alarm. The open window provides ample ventilation."

I sighed and gazed about at the cluttered room in paranoia. "With your unhealthy obsession for chemistry, I felt a bit safer in this house knowing that there was a working fire alarm in here."

Holmes chuckled. "Don't fret, Watson. I assume you didn't come to my room at dawn for idle *bavardage*."

"Did they catch her?" I asked eagerly.

227

"Yes, the police picked her up near the Richardsons' home last night. I am staying out of the official investigation, although I did report my findings at the police station last night. I had worked out most of the details, but a few points needed clarifying. I wasn't able to talk to Roksanda, but I got what I needed since Mr. Richardson is good friends with the chief of police."

"You can start at the beginning." I sat down at the desk and took a large gulp of my now-cool tea. I realized too late that the skull was staring at me. Holmes began his tale, completely unaware of my predicament.

"From the very start, this problem had a number of features of interest. An anthropologist of affluence, Dr. Aurelia Richardson, embarks on an expedition and has a mental breakdown, which results in the death of her colleague and graduate students. She is institutionalized, and after spending six years in such a state, she is allowed to return home under a nurse's supervision. For many months, all is fine and the patient appears well, and then suddenly, there is a reversal in health — hallucinations, paranoia, and even suicide attempts. The housekeeper, Roksanda, fearing that Mr. Richardson was in denial about the declining state of his daughter, approaches a long-time friend of her mother's, Mrs. H, for help with convincing him to do the right thing. And that is where we entered. Hours later, the housekeeper is proven correct when Dr. Richardson allegedly attacks the woman who practically raised her. An unremarkable story at first glance, Watson, but there is more to this than meets the eye."

I heartily disagreed—nothing about what happened to Aurelia Richardson was unremarkable—but my curiosity begged for my silence, and I obliged.

"Do you recall our conversation with Mr. Richardson on the landing?" Holmes asked. "As we went downstairs, three possible solutions came to mind based on the data he provided. One, Dr. Richardson's health was declining, and no unnatural forces were at work. Her medication, for instance, may have lost its effectiveness. Two, as Mrs. H later vaguely hinted, supernatural forces were at work—that is to say, our victim was being tormented by one or more ghosts. Three, a perpetrator of flesh and bone was somehow instigating Dr. Richardson's present state.

"The first I dismissed almost immediately. Mr. Richardson may be reluctant to part with his money to heat or secure the house, but it was easy to tell he adored his daughter. She was undoubtedly getting the best treatment money could buy. If her medication was becoming ineffective, her doctors would have noticed. The second theory was quite far-fetched, but every solution must be considered. However, as the case progressed, I was able to dismiss diabolical interference simply because evidence for the third theory manifested."

"The humerus?" I asked.

Holmes nodded. "Yes, very good, Watson. Remember how Roksanda was poking around Dr. Richardson's dig spot yesterday? Note that she was using her foot. Yet I spotted dirt on her fingers when she joined us a minute later. Had she also used her hand to sift through the dirt, or had she picked up something dirty? I grew suspicious then. The truth was that Dr. Richardson had indeed spotted a humerus but was quickly discredited since Roksanda managed to throw the bone over the stone wall without being noticed. She is a stealthy one, I must admit."

"So she was trying to make it look like Aurelia was imagining things?" I cried. "Does that mean she planted the bone there?"

Holmes smirked. "Do lower your volume, Watson. Other people live here after all."

I ignored the mocking reprimand. "Then she must've also been the one who left the rope on the landing. How could she try to k-kill Aurelia!"

My friend grew grave as he said, "It is a wicked world, but no, she was not that wicked. I examined the rope and the way it had been tied to the handrail. Had Aurelia thrown herself off, the rope would have become untied, and her neck would not have snapped. The fall may have broken a bone or two, but it would not have killed her."

"So Roksanda wanted to hurt Aurelia but not kill her?"

"Hurt her enough to have her hospitalized."

"But why?"

"I had no idea then, but it became clear as the investigation progressed. Allow me to backtrack a bit and resume the narrative from the yard scene. As the party made its way back to the kitchen, I left the property via the backyard. You may recall Aurora saying that the property backs onto a park? That is where the bone had landed. I retrieved it and entered the house through the front to avoid detection. Luckily, the door was unlocked since we did not lock it after letting ourselves in."

"But wouldn't Roksanda have gone looking for the bone afterwards?" I asked. "Did she ever suspect you'd taken it?

"No, I believe not," Holmes replied, shaking his head. "She may have searched the park at the end of her shift, but probably assumed it had been taken by a dog or kids. Anyway, I came back into the house and found the library by happenstance, hid the bone there, and then made my way back to you. My objective from then on was to discover Roksanda's motive and find first-hand evidence. I suspected she had used various tricks to induce Dr. Richardson's episodes. The poor woman in her vulnerable state could be deceived simply by suggestibility.

231

In fact, Roksanda unwittingly admitted that Dr. Richardson began digging in the yard the day after she had been left in charge of her. Who knows what she might have said to provoke such behaviour! But it was only the beginning.

"I was rather on edge the night we spent at the Richardson house. I dismissed Mrs. H's paranoia, but the more I thought about it, that night would have been perfect for Roksanda to strike — to hurt Dr. Richardson badly. With Mr. and Mrs. Richardson out of the way, there would only be three people in the house. She could let herself in after everyone was asleep and carry out an attack against Dr. Richardson. The realization unnerved me, Watson, although I had not an ounce of proof that something would happen."

"So you kept watch by the window."

"Indeed. But I fell asleep! And then something I had never expected came to pass — Mrs. H was attacked instead. I was both grief-stricken and bewildered. If I hadn't fallen asleep, Mrs. H would not be in a hospital bed right now. I could have stopped — "

"That wasn't your fault. Try not to beat yourself up over it," I said sympathetically.

Holmes sighed. "I thought I had mostly solved the mystery, but here was another, more terrible one. I now had to discover if the attack was an isolated event or if it was somehow related to the events surrounding Dr. Richardson. Personally, I couldn't imagine

Roksanda viciously stabbing her mother's old friend, but I let the evidence speak for itself.

"By examining the front and back door locks, I could tell that the perpetrator didn't force their way in. Furthermore, there was the shoe print that had not been there before. Although it was partial, it was small—a woman's shoe. I surmised that the culprit had entered the house through the back door and taken off their shoes in order to move about the house as quietly as possible. The spot of the attack and the crooked painting were the next set of clues."

The melancholy from moments ago faded a little and Holmes spoke excitedly. "As I mentioned to you before, the scene of the crime was most suggestive. The culprit didn't attempt to hide when they heard Mrs. H coming downstairs, even though they could have easily done so. Now, what would prompt someone to behave in such a manner? I thought that perhaps they had been occupied with a task; if they had hidden, their intentions would have still come to light via Mrs. H. In this case, a large sum of money was involved, so our culprit was quite reluctant to leave the job unfinished."

"But what's in that hallway that's worth a lot of money?" I exclaimed. "Wait—one of the paintings? Aurelia's painting! And the culprit—it turned out to be Roksanda after all?"

"Yes. Roksanda was in the process of removing the painting and replacing it with a duplicate she had painted when Mrs. H interrupted her. She could have run out the patio door and saved herself, but she had taken the painting off the wall at that point. Had she fled, the burglary would have been discovered, and the Richardsons, wondering why someone wanted to nick something they had considered worthless, might have even consulted an appraisal service. If the painting's true value had been realized, then all would be lost. Hence, she took the risk and decided to confront the approaching person."

I was dumbfounded. "All this happened over a painting?"

"Not just any painting. One allegedly by Tom Thomson—you know the name surely. Ah, judging by the expression on your face, I reckon you are aware that he was an artist, but know nothing else? Did they not cover art and history in school? Surely you must be familiar with his works, *The Jack Pine* and *The West*—no? I am not sure if the school system or your poor memory is to blame here. I seem to know more about your country's history than you do."

In my defence, Holmes knew more about every country's history than the average citizen, but such a declaration would have elevated his already high sense of self-regard, so I simply scowled.

"The details are fresh in my mind, thanks to my visit to the art gallery. Tom Thomson—one of the country's most influential painters of the 20th century, born 1877. Although he burned much of his work, quite a collection remains, despite his untimely death at age thirty-nine, and is worth a tidy sum. A recent discovery, for instance, sold in auction for nearly half a million dollars.

"You can imagine how Roksanda had felt, stumbling across such a find. A meagre salary, burdened by student loans, unable to find a job in her field, and surrounded by the opulence of the Richardson home every day—now that is a recipe for crime! Stealing from so wealthy a family didn't seem wrong to her, but unfortunately for her, Mrs. Richardson took a liking to the painting and insisted on having it framed. Otherwise, Roksanda could have easily nicked the work, and her employers would have been none the wiser. She still didn't want to do anything overt, which was why she now had the added step of creating a duplicate and swapping the paintings.

"It took her nearly two months to make the forgery, and by late August, it was ready for the swap. The trouble was that she could find no opportune time to carry out the task. Someone was always home and this was due mostly to Dr. Richardson's presence. She seldom left the house and often roamed around, accompanied by Alejo. Even Mr. Richardson was working from home more to be near his daughter. It, therefore, became her sole goal to evict Dr. Richardson from the house, and so began her torture. What we witnessed in the yard became a common tactic of hers, and her victim's nerves shattered accordingly."

"But even though Aurelia got worse, Mr. Richardson refused to have her institutionalized, which was why she approached Mrs. Hudson for help, hoping that she could convince him," I said.

Holmes nodded. "For once, Mrs. H's superstitious mindset proved useful. Had she not suspected supernatural players to be at work, she may have never asked us to become involved."

"She also wouldn't have been viciously attacked."

"Ah, well, yes, dreadful business that. One shove against the wall and Mrs. H had lost consciousness, but she was still very much alive and could identify the culprit. Roksanda became desperate and decided to frame Dr. Richardson. Aware of how Dr. Richardson had killed her colleague and graduate students six years before, she borrowed a knife from the kitchen and did the deed. She then proceeded upstairs and placed the weapon in Dr. Richardson's hands. She probably wore gloves, so I doubt the police will find her prints anywhere incriminating. Luckily, she made a grave error on her way downstairs."

"She stepped on the blood."

"Quite so. The blood trail was most telling. The shape of the spots, as well as the distance between them, told me the perpetrator had ascended the stairs at a normal walking pace. The smudged speck told me the culprit would have blood on their sock. I also knew that the sock had been immediately taken off since there was no additional blood transferred to the steps from the sock. I checked Dr. Richardson's feet just to be sure, but I was certain Roksanda's involvement in the first crime was somehow tied to the second. Finding the sock was the key to solving the case, but I had no idea where Roksanda had hidden it or if she had already disposed of it.

"The next day while you were in class, I took a walk around the neighbourhood, checking all the garbage bins along the way, but that yielded nothing. I hoped the sock was safe somewhere in Roksanda's home, and my plan was to follow her after she finished work since neither Mr. Richardson nor Aurora seemed to remember her home address." He shook his head in annoyance. "In the meantime, I decided to do some research on the artwork that had led to such an unfortunate series of events by visiting the art gallery. That was where I came across the collection of Thomson paintings. The technique, colour choice, and subject were remarkably similar, and I began to wonder if the crooked painting was a Thomson. To confirm that it was the source of all this misery, I took a picture and showed it to Dr. Richardson, whose sharp eye picked up Roksanda's copy. The pieces finally fell into place, Watson.

"You can now understand why I was in such a hurry to head back to the Richardsons' after our visit to the police station. I needed to catch Roksanda before she left. Unfortunately, she was smarter than me. She had disposed of the sock in the fireplace before we arrived, hence the smell of burning wool. I was stumped and quite angry with myself—even you had noticed my bothered state, Watson."

An indignant response made my tongue quiver—I too was capable of noticing things—but I swallowed it. Curiosity had conquered my pride. Holmes went on, oblivious to my irritation; his voice grew very excited.

"But then Aurora spilled soup on her blouse and the stains made me realize something. Roksanda had not carried the sock home in her hand; she must have put it somewhere. Only the pocket of her trousers would have been available to her while standing on the stairs. The blood could have transferred from sock to pocket, and she would have been none the wiser. There was my evidence, Watson, which I found with your help, of course. That, along with the stolen painting, is irrefutable evidence of Roksanda's guilt."

The credit appeased me somewhat. "Yesterday, when you tricked her into telling us about Aurelia's past, I thought you were just eager to find out what Aurelia had done. But I was also confused when you stopped me from questioning Aurora about it. Now I understand that you were trying to see if Roksanda knew what was supposed to be a well-kept secret. Even Mrs. Hudson probably didn't know."

"I agree. The poor woman had no idea what she was walking into."

"Well, I'm glad that business is done with. I'll come with you to see Mrs. Hudson if you're going today."

"Actually, I went to see her after I finished up at the police station yesterday. Visiting hours were over, so I was initially planning to sneak past the nurses' station. But since I needed to gain admittance to find out how Mrs. H was doing, I ended up telling them I was her grandson. Had to spin quite a tale to convince them, but I prevailed in the end." He looked very pleased with himself.

"They probably just got tired of hearing you ramble," I muttered disapprovingly. "So how is she doing?"

"Still unconscious, but stable."

"But the phone call—" I stammered. "You said she was awake."

"I already told you that the phone call was a ruse. It was a personal call, unrelated to this case, but your ability to jump to conclusions allowed me to take advantage of it. I congratulate you, Watson, although, in the end, it didn't really help."

"But why did you lie?"

"My original plan was to have you lure Roksanda back to the house while I searched her room, but after the call and your most brilliant assumption, I changed my plans in order to make the housekeeper become desperate. If Mrs. H could talk, she could identify her attacker. I predicted Roksanda would immediately try to flee with the painting at hand, and I would be there to catch her. But she didn't try to escape; her nerves had become too frazzled. In her panicked state, she had no idea what to do, so I had to revert to my original plan in order to draw her out."

"I thought she sounded a bit shaken on the phone," I recalled. "I can't believe she hurt Mrs. Hudson over a painting. How did she even know for sure the painting was the real deal?"

"I learned the answer to that at the police station," Holmes said. "There was a document accompanying the painting, addressed to Mr. Richardson's father, which outlined the sale of a Tom Thomson painting that had been found in the painter's studio, which by happenstance is only a few minutes' walk from here—a remarkable coincidence, isn't it? The sale was dated to 1920. Roksanda hid the document, of course, and she alone knew the work's provenance, but it was all for naught."

"What do you mean?"

"After Thomson's death in 1917, which was a mystery in itself—I will let you read up on that later—a large number of sketches and paintings remained in his studio that was not signed or dated. Two years later, J.E.H. MacDonald, artist, friend, and colleague of Thomson, designed a stamp, consisting of the initials 'TT' and the date '1917' to authenticate these works.

"According to the letter Roksanda found, the painting had been found in the studio. Yet when I examined the painting, there was no sign of a stamp. Hence, a forgery. Mr. Richardson's father had probably reached the same conclusion sometime after the purchase, which was why it sat neglected in the basement all this time."

"I see," I murmured, feeling disheartened. I was not an art enthusiast, yet the prospect of unearthing a new discovery had excited even me. I took a sip of cold tea and reluctantly swallowed. "There's one thing you've missed, Holmes."

My friend looked amused. "Care to enlighten me then?"

"Roksanda's accomplice."

"Are you referring to Alejo?"

My shoulders drooped rather dramatically, which elicited a toothy grin from Holmes. It was difficult to hide my disappointment that he had made the same realization as I. Perhaps my suspicion that Alejo had been Roksanda's accomplice was an obvious one. His "smoking break" lie and mysterious disappearance could be explained in no other way. I was certain he lent the housekeeper a hand, providing anything she needed to scare Aurelia, like the rope. Why he had saved her from the painful fall intrigued me though.

"It is not an entirely ridiculous assumption, mate," Holmes said, interrupting my reverie. "The timing of Alejo Santos' disappearance is most suspicious, and I assure you something criminal is at work. However, it is not as nefarious as the case we have just closed."

Intrigued, I waited for him to go on.

"Do you recall Roksanda's odd statement about Alejo? 'He could be standing right in front of me, but he doesn't respond.' Quite a curious thing, wouldn't you say? Either he was becoming deaf, which I have disproven already, or something else was at work. What would prompt a person not to turn around when called? Think, Watson, think!"

Under his unblinking scrutiny, I failed to respond. How was one supposed to think in the midst of smoke, icy air, and a grinning skull? Holmes grew impatient as he usually did and answered his own question.

"One would not respond if one were accustomed to another name. I surmised that Alejo Santos is not the nurse's real name, that perhaps he is here illegally, and that he was hired by Mr. Richardson for well below the salary of a live-in nurse. Naturally, the man fled when there was talk of police. I confronted Mr. Richardson while at the police station last night, in whispered tones, of course, and he has confirmed my theory. I think it is best to let that matter be."

"But he lied about the smoke break! He obviously set up the rope and led Aurelia to it."

"He didn't lie, Watson. Alejo did indeed step out for a smoke. He used the balcony in Dr. Richardson's room. I found cigarette ash smudged on the floor. Luckily, he stepped on the ash on his way back in, so it didn't get blown away by the wind. In fact, I recognized the brand—"

"I'm sure you did," I interrupted. "You can write a paper on all the varieties of cigarette ash out there some day. Back to the case—was this the second case you were talking about?"

"Of course not. It was the third. Have you forgotten the missing jewellery?"

"But that was Aurelia—"

"That most certainly was not. Dr. Richardson has no interest in jewellery. Her life's work revolved around the history of humanity and traces of the past, not shiny stones. Didn't the state of the yard reveal that clearly? No, someone of sound mind, someone with an appetite for spending but had little means—they took the jewellery."

Only one name came to my mind. "Aurora?"

"Indeed! She is a thief and a liar. For starters, she is not pregnant. It was simply an excuse to move back home; no one would deny a pregnant woman who had been shunned by her husband, not even Mrs. Richardson, who probably was not very happy to have both of her husband's adult daughters in the house."

I was more startled by this than the news of Alejo's double identity. Aurora had seemed so...pregnant. The glow in her cheeks, the protective way she cradled her belly—Holmes was either mistaken or Aurora was a splendid actress. It turned out neither was true.

"How did you know she wasn't pregnant?" I asked.

"The signs were obvious from the very start," Holmes answered matter-of-factly. "A pregnant woman knows better than to go to a sushi bar or plan to relax in a sauna. Foods like sushi can be challenging for the immune system and overheating can be dangerous for the baby; it cannot sweat, and thus, doesn't have the capability to cool down in the womb. Aurora clearly had no idea what pregnancy entails; she was putting on an act without having done the research. I realized right away. And I think Roksanda did too but didn't know how to expose her, and that resulted in the animosity we witnessed between the two ladies. This was why I cautioned you not to use Aurora's pregnancy as an excuse to lure Roksanda out of her rooms. I suspect Mrs. H knew as well. With her years of wisdom, she detected the sham, but chose not to intervene. Love excuses a great many silly things, I suppose."

"But why fake the pregnancy?" I asked.

"Her husband lost his job at the fancy law firm he worked at, but that did not prompt the Giordanos to reduce their expenditures. Poverty befell them and the couple hatched a plan to pay off their debts by stealing. Frugal as Mr. Richardson is, he would never have given them a handout. Hence, the theatrics. It was not a very clever plan, however. I have no idea how Aurora planned to explain having no baby in the end."

"And how did you find out all of this?"

"I confronted Aurora yesterday morning before my walk. She supplied the details without much persuasion. I think all the work associated with putting on the act was starting to become tiresome for her. I took advantage of her talkative mood and accused her of taking the jewellery in order to assess her reaction. She protested at first, but then divulged all. In fact, she seemed somewhat relieved after our discussion and has promised to tell her father everything."

"Amazing. You're — I mean, all of this is just amazing."

Holmes beamed. "Elementary."

"You seem to have accomplished quite a lot while I was sitting in class," I said grudgingly, although I couldn't help but admire the genius of the man before me. Never would I admit this out loud though; Holmes was sensitive to flattery when it concerned his "art". Complimenting his intellect would only motivate him to laugh harder the next time I blundered.

His response was kinder than my thoughts. "You are fretting again, Watson. Don't be so hard on yourself."

"I didn't help solve the case in any way."

"You may not possess genius, my friend, but you have the remarkable power of stimulating it."

"Uh, thank you, I guess."

"It was meant as a compliment."

I set my mug down and leaned in. "You have a funny way of complimenting people, but putting that aside for now, I need one final explanation from you. The shadow I saw on the landing just as we entered the foyer—was that Roksanda?"

"Alas, the evidence says no."

Too stunned to respond, all I could do was stare incredulously and allow Holmes to continue.

"Roksanda had left the house before we exited our room," he explained. "In fact, I am quite sure in her nervous state, she let the patio door bang shut on her way out. That was the sound that woke me up. If Roksanda had run upstairs, having heard us in the hallway, there would be evidence for that—remember that the shape and spread of the drops of blood on the steps were indicative of a person walking up the stairs. It is quite implausible when you think about it. We raised the alarm quickly after finding Mrs. H. Roksanda would have had no chance to sneak out of the house."

"But I'm sure I saw something up there."

In response, Holmes' eyes twinkled—with a hint of mischief, I thought. "I believe your imagination is the culprit here—a phantasm perhaps. In the off chance that what you witnessed was indeed forces outside the ordinary laws of nature, I would say the best course of action is to let it be. Such a realm is beyond the power of the blood-and-flesh detective, my dear Watson."

About the Author

Jia Hartsiva currently works in academic publishing and lives with her family in Toronto, Canada. She has previously written for the business and popular science fields, although her heart lies in the world of fiction. She has a weakness for whodunits and a passion for Sherlock Holmes. *The Arrival of Sherlock Holmes* is her first novel of the great detective.

Visit www.trulyholmes.ca to learn more.